UNDONE BY HIS TOUCH

UNDONE BY HIS TOUCH

BY
ANNIE WEST

All the characters in this book have no existence
outside the imagination of the author, and have
no relation whatsoever to anyone bearing the same
name or names. They are not even distantly inspired
by any individual known or unknown to the author,
and all the incidents are pure invention.

First published in Great Britain 2012
by Mills & Boon, an imprint of Harlequin (UK) Limited.
Large Print edition 2012
Harlequin (UK) Limited, Eton House,
18-24 Paradise Road, Richmond, Surrey TW9 1SR

© Annie West 2012

ISBN: 978 0 263 22601 0

Harlequin (UK) policy is to use papers that are natural,
renewable and recyclable products and made from
wood grown in sustainable forests. The logging and
manufacturing process conform to the legal environmental
regulations of the country of origin.

Printed and bound in Great Britain
by CPI Antony Rowe, Chippenham, Wiltshire

PROLOGUE

'YOU can't save us!' The hoarse cry echoed in Declan's ears and he tore his gaze back to Adrian, dangling below him on the rope. 'It's going to give way!'

They were suspended a hundred metres above an isolated canyon. The wind was rising and his brother's nerves were shot. Already Adrian's panic had dislodged one of the pitons securing them to the cliff.

'Hang on,' Declan gasped. His lungs hammered from his last attempt to haul them up.

Craning his neck, he looked up to where they'd fallen. A cascade of crumbling rock splattered his face. His throat shredded raw with each breath.

If only he'd called Adrian's bluff when he'd threatened to climb solo. But Adrian had seemed so brittle, Declan hadn't pushed. He'd hoped to re-gain their closeness and persuade Adrian to open up while they climbed.

Now their survival hung in the balance.

'Steady, Ade. It'll be OK.'

'OK?' Adrian's voice rose. 'Don't lie, Declan.'

Declan shot him a reassuring look. 'I almost made it last time. Third time's the charm. You'll see.'

Setting his jaw, he grabbed the rope and hauled, blocking out screaming pain as the rope lacerated hands already raw. His shoulders and neck locked in agony as he took their combined weight. It felt as if his spine might snap or his shoulders dislocate from the strain.

'You'll never do it. It's impossible.'

The words washed over him. He had no wind for speech.

'You know, it's not so bad.' Minutes later Adrian spoke again, his voice barely audible over the thundering of Declan's blood. 'A fall will be quick, at least.'

'Won't…' Declan fought to dredge up words in a throat scoured dry '…fall.'

'I've thought about it. One turn of the wheel in front of an oncoming truck and it'd all be over.'

The words slurred, warped by the frantic throb of Declan's pulse and the searing pain in his hands. Sweat blurred his vision.

'It's not like there's anything to live for.' Adrian's

voice was so soft Declan wasn't sure if he imagined it. Could pain make you hallucinate?

'I've lost her. She wants someone rich and successful like you, not a failure. She dumped me!'

'Dumped?' Declan's voice was a husk of sound.

He needed to stop before his arms wrenched from their sockets. The world narrowed to the line that wore his hands to the bone, the wrenching strain and the eddying sound of Adrian's voice. A shiver of anxiety snaked through him at his brother's tone, but he was too exhausted to respond.

The wind picked up, swaying them.

The salt tang of blood burst on his lip. Two metres…

'I can't go on. I've tried, but she's the only woman I ever loved and she betrayed me. This is for the best.'

Best? The rope jerked unevenly. Despite the sweat streaming over Declan's sun-baked body, an icy finger slicked the back of his neck.

'Ade?'

Readjusting frozen neck muscles, he managed to look down. Familiar grey eyes met his. This time they held no panic, only an odd calm that made Declan's heart plunge.

'This way one of us might survive. I can't go on without her.'

Declan gasped in horror as he looked lower to where Adrian sawed at the line that bound them.

'Adrian! No!'

'Goodbye, Declan.'

Suddenly the dragging weight on his shoulders disappeared. There was no scream, no sound. It seemed a lifetime before Declan heard the muffled crunch of branches below and lost sight of his brother.

CHAPTER ONE

THE stack of towels was thick and soft in Chloe's arms as she nudged open the laundry door and headed for the pool house.

She dipped her head and inhaled the scent of sunshine and lavender: one of the special touches she prided herself on when the weather was good enough to use the drying hedge rather than the industrial-sized drier.

Concentrating on such small things, resuming her routine, had seen her through this difficult first morning back at Carinya.

She refused to let memories spook her. Her job was too precious and she needed the financial security more than ever. Besides, she had nothing to fear now.

So she'd ignored the anxiety feathering down her spine when she'd entered her housekeeper's quarters and remembered the last morning she'd been here. And again as she'd started work and imagined a dark-haired presence watching from the shadows as he had so often watched before.

That was in the past. He'd gone for ever. That knowledge helped banish the shadows.

Turning the corner of the house she slowed, hearing the sound of someone in the pool.

The sight of a familiar dark head emerging from the water with each stroke slammed her heart against her ribs. She faltered to a stop, not believing her eyes.

But he's gone!

This was impossible!

Transfixed, Chloe watched him execute a perfect racing turn, coming up metres from the end of the pool. The strenuous butterfly stroke, one she'd never been able to master, looked easy as that long body cleaved the water. The scoop of out-thrust arms accentuated the impressive length of tanned limbs and the power in his shoulders.

Chloe sagged against the wall, her throat tight, heart pounding as she tried to make sense of what she saw.

But he's dead... Dead. The words ran, a bewildered mantra, through her brain.

Yet for one lap of the pool Chloe was caught in nightmare, transfixed by the return of the man she'd come to fear.

Another turn and this time he swam freestyle, powering down the metres as if he had a record to break.

It was only then that her stunned eyes saw beyond the shreds of memory and noticed anomalies. This man looked bigger, though it was difficult to tell in the water. He swam differently, as if propelled by an unseen force that supercharged him through the crystal depths. He was like an efficient machine, each stroke smooth and economical, yet with a raw strength that seemed almost brutal.

Chloe couldn't imagine this man doing a lazy lap or two then loafing away an afternoon at the poolside with a tray of drinks and his mobile phone.

Even now, turning again and beginning another lap, his speed didn't diminish.

Driven: that was the word that came to mind.

The man she remembered had been many things but driven wasn't one of them. *At least, not until he'd turned his attention to her.*

Chloe clanged that door shut in her mind. She refused to go there.

The swimmer reached the far end of the pool and in one supple movement heaved himself out. Water streamed down, bright sunlight burnished bronzed, water-slicked skin, from the bunch of muscles in his arms and back to the tight curve of bare buttocks.

Chloe sucked in her breath, her dazed brain registering his nakedness at the same time it assured her this couldn't be *him*. The shape of the head was different. The height. The breadth. His sheer imposing *maleness*.

He half-turned and she averted her eyes, but not before she saw a long scar ripping down one powerful thigh.

Relief, the return to normality after those frozen moments of disbelief, made her light-headed. Sanity returned with a rush of embarrassment as she realised who she'd been staring at.

Hurriedly, she straightened away from the wall and stepped out briskly towards the pool house.

'Who's that?' The deep voice was sharp but he didn't turn around, merely reached for his towel on a nearby sun lounger. He wrapped it casually round his hips with all the nonchalance of a man supremely confident in his own nakedness. And the fact he owned the whole multi-million-dollar estate.

Reluctantly Chloe detoured towards the clematis-draped pergola where he stood, putting on sunglasses.

It wasn't the way she'd have chosen to meet her employer at last.

Housekeepers were supposed to be discreet, unobtrusive, not intruding on their boss's privacy.

The image of firmly toned masculine flesh flashed before her eyes and a tingle of unfamiliar heat stirred.

She faltered, taking a moment to identify the sensation she hadn't experienced in years. When she did, shock brought a gasp to her lips.

'I'm waiting.' The words weren't curt, but his languid tone barely concealed impatience.

Chloe stepped forward. Now was not the time to dwell on the fact she'd just felt a spark of arousal for the first time in six years. At the sight of her naked employer.

'It's your housekeeper, Chloe Daniels.' She waited for him to turn. When he finally did she hefted the towels higher on one arm and extended her right hand. Tried to banish the memory of how she'd stood, gawping like some sex-starved miss at the sight of him.

Sex-starved she might technically be but she was no simpering miss.

He stood four-square before her, wearing nothing but reflective sunglasses and a towel. He exuded an air of authority that befitted a man of his commercial stature.

Right now it was his physical stature that pole-axed her.

Chloe had to tilt her head to meet his eyes. Despite her self-discipline and the compelling need not to ogle her employer, it took far too much effort to keep her gaze from that broad chest and ridged abdomen.

Standing this close, she realised Declan Carstairs was bigger, tougher, more imposing than the man she'd known. Only the hair colour and loose-limbed grace were the same—family traits.

His jaw was shadowed, not with sculpted designer stubble, but with several days' growth that made him look more like a lumberjack or pirate than a corporate tycoon.

A sensation like swirling treacle low in her belly unnerved her. She had a sudden mental picture of him swinging across a tall-masted ship, a woman on his shoulder.

Maybe it was the scar that conjured the notion. Long and not yet silvered with age, it carved an uncompromising groove up one cheek, curling in towards his eye.

Chloe shivered as she thought of the long matching wound on his leg.

'We haven't met before,' she said in the efficient housekeeper's voice she'd perfected over the years. She was grateful for it now as her pulse hammered. 'I've been—'

'Away.' He paused, watching her, yet giving no answering smile. His forehead pleated in a frown and his dark eyebrows slashed down as if in disapproval.

By now she felt gauche with her arm extended towards him. When it became clear he wouldn't give her the courtesy of a handshake, she dropped her arm, disappointment adding to her discomfort. Maybe arrogance ran in his family.

'A family emergency, wasn't it?' he surprised her by asking.

She hadn't expected him to know that, especially since they'd never met. His personal assistant had hired her, explaining his boss was often away for months at a time. Carinya had been his family's spectacular Blue Mountains retreat for generations but he lived a couple of hours east in Sydney when he wasn't travelling.

'That's right, Mr Carstairs. A family issue.'

Not that she'd known that the morning she'd fled this house. She'd simply packed her bags and caught the first train out. It was only later she'd discovered that in a weird coincidence of fate she faced not one but two crises. At least one of them was over.

'But we can count on your continued presence now?' One eyebrow arched above sleek designer glasses.

'Of course.' She'd been grateful when her sudden request for leave had been granted, but now she felt a spark of resentment at his attitude. 'I moved back in a couple of hours ago. I'll be on hand whenever you need me.' She forced herself to smile up into his stern face.

If she'd expected a glimmer of friendliness she was disappointed.

The way he stood, staring, no answering smile or nod, should have unnerved her. But Chloe was used to standing up for herself, proving herself again and again. Her self-confidence had been forged in a hard school.

She met his gaze squarely, trying to read his face.

Most people gave non-verbal clues to their thoughts. Not Declan Carstairs. Maybe that was how he'd taken his inherited fortune and turned it into something astronomical—by playing his cards close to his chest.

Yet this was something more. Was that disapproval she read in his set jaw and tense mouth? Anger, even?

Her skin tightened as she recalled standing frozen, eyes glued to his naked form, well after she'd realised who he was. There'd been a distinct element of appreciation as her gaze had slid over his virile form.

Had he caught her staring? Heat washed her throat and cheeks.

'I'm sorry for interrupting you just now. I hadn't realised you were here in the pool.'

Or that you were naked.

'Mr Sarkesian left a message saying you'd both be working in your study this morning and he'd brief me after that. I'd never intentionally…'

A dismissive gesture silenced her. 'David had to leave on unexpected business.' He paused and she had the impression of tension clamping his big frame rigid. 'Was there anything else?'

'No, nothing.' She'd been waiting for *him*. 'I'll just take these to the pool house. Unless there's anything I can get you?'

He shook his head. Chloe fought not to notice the way tiny droplets of water eased over his shoulders to track down across the solid musculature of his chest.

Her mouth dried and the heat in her face notched up to scorching.

She was doing it again!

She didn't ogle attractive men. Yet the sight of her boss's half-naked body and don't-mess-with-me jaw conjured feelings Chloe had all but forgotten. How could it be?

Even the dreadful scar seemed to accentuate the earthy sexuality and power of his strong-boned face.

Inwardly she cringed, hoping he was oblivious to her thoughts tumbling out of control.

That black eyebrow climbed again. 'Well. What are you waiting for, Ms Daniels? Don't let me keep you from work.'

That was what he paid her for. She had no trouble reading his dismissive tone.

'Of course, Mr Carstairs.' Chloe tamped down annoyance and embarrassment as she turned away. She kept her pace even and her shoulders back, projecting a calm she was far from feeling.

Yet she reeled in shock. First had been the horror of thinking the man who haunted her nightmares had returned. Then there'd been that rush of relief, so strong she'd trembled with it. And finally the punch-to-the-gut reaction to Declan Carstairs.

Despite the scarring, he had the body of a male

pin-up. More than that his sheer, sizzling intensity resonated like a force field, sucking the air from her lungs.

She was horrified to register a jiggle of response in that secret hollow place deep within. It had been years since she'd felt sexual awareness. On the contrary, she'd been accused of chilling indifference, of being an ice princess.

The recollection twisted her lips. She'd promised herself never to dwell on that again.

Now to feel a spark of attraction for her boss? Impossible!

In twenty-seven years there'd only been Mark, just one man to make her feel the blaze of desire. It was unthinkable that Declan Carstairs, rich, ruthless and disapproving, should reignite such feelings.

Pursing her lips, Chloe set about stripping the pool house of used towels.

Halfway back to the house, the sound of shattering glass made her spin towards the pergola.

Declan Carstairs stood, frozen in tableau, one arm stretched towards the table. On the ground before him lay the splintered remnants of a glass.

Curiously it was his stillness that snared her gaze rather than the broken glass so dangerously close to the pool. Too late she caught herself staring at those broad, straight shoulders a little too avidly.

'It's all right, Mr Carstairs, don't you bother with it. I'll fetch a brush and pan.' Chloe hurried back to the laundry, dumped the towels and scooped up her equipment.

Strangely, on her return he hadn't moved, as if he was waiting to make sure she did the job properly.

She'd worked for wealthy people before, some demanding and others so relaxed they barely noticed what went on around them. None would have questioned her ability to do such a simple task. Yet his stillness and the furrow of concentration on his brow told her he had other ideas.

Chloe crouched before him, brushing up the shards.

'I'll just be a moment.' Yet her usually brisk movements seemed slow, her limbs heavy as his silent presence loomed close. Deliberately she turned from the sight of those strong sinewed feet planted wide on the flagstones.

Ridiculous that even the man's naked feet looked sexy. He disapproved of her, was checking on her. She didn't want to feel anything for him.

'Thank you, Ms Daniels.'

Chloe bit down on a bubble of laughter. Such formality when her mind buzzed with unsettling images of his bare body. Just as well he couldn't read her thoughts.

If only he'd move and leave her to get on with this.

Thinning her lips, she concentrated on locating shards that had spread further than the rest. 'I think that's almost— No! Watch out!'

Too late she saw his heel come down on a splinter as he turned.

A single, low oath blasted from his lips as bright scarlet bloomed and spread across the flagstones.

'Wait, there's another one.'

Chloe scuttled across to pick up the shard. 'There, that's all. You can move to the chair now.'

Above her he stood still as a bronze god, though in the silence she heard the hiss of his indrawn breath. Blood streamed from the gash at his heel.

Finally he spoke. 'Perhaps you'd help me, Ms Daniels.'

Frowning, she got to her feet, put the brush and pan aside and moved closer. What did he want her to do? Surely he had the strength to hop the short distance to the chair?

'You want me to support you?'

Something like anger flashed across his face and his nostrils flared. 'Nothing so dramatic.' He spoke through gritted teeth. 'Just give me your hand.'

Bewildered, Chloe complied, slipping her hand into his, absorbing the heat and sensation of hard strength surrounding her work-roughened fingers. She registered the ridges of scar tissue across his palm. A shiver of sensation skated up her arm and shoulder, raising the fine hairs on her nape.

She ignored it and looked into his face. This close she read the tiny lines bracketing his mouth as if he spent more time compressing his lips than smiling.

His features were stiff and the scar stood lividly on his taut cheek. Fierce energy hummed through him and into her, like a power source without a safety valve, inexorably rising. Tension twisted as she waited for him to speak.

Her eyes were at the level of his mouth and she watched, fascinated, as his sensuously sculpted lips thinned into a pained line.

'You need to sit down so I can get the glass out. It won't hurt so much then.'

His bark of laughter, rough and raw, echoed across the flagstones, jerking her gaze up to those impenetrable dark glasses.

'The pain doesn't bother me.'

Chloe frowned. If he wasn't in pain, then what…?

He exhaled slowly through his nostrils, his fingers tightening around hers. When he spoke there was resignation as well as an undercurrent of anger in his words. 'Just lead me to a chair, will you?'

'Lead…?'

'Yes, damn it. Haven't you realised you're talking to a blind man?'

CHAPTER TWO

THE silence pounded with the beat of blood roaring in his ears. He held his breath with anticipation, waiting for the inevitable gush of sympathy.

It was all he could do not to fling away from her. He didn't want sympathy. He didn't want company. But he couldn't afford the luxury of managing for himself. He'd probably end up with a foot full of glass, or, having lost his bearings completely, a black eye from walking into the pergola.

Almost he didn't care. Yet he retained enough pride not to want to make a complete fool of himself before her. He did that often enough when he was alone.

Frustration surged and his muscles tightened as he thought of his frequent tumbles, his inability to do half the things he'd always taken for granted.

'Of course,' she murmured. 'I apologise. I hadn't realised you couldn't see.' Her words were the same as before, cool, crisp, not a shred of syrupy sympathy and for a moment he stood, startled.

Then she lifted his arm, wrapped hers around his torso and wedged her shoulder beneath his armpit. 'If you lean on me it will be easier.'

She might have been a nurse with her brisk practicality. If he was reasonable he'd be grateful for her no-nonsense attitude.

But the soft press of her breast against his side, the cushioned swell of her hip against his thigh, the sudden scent of vanilla and sunshine as her hair tickled his bare chest and arm, made him anything but reasonable.

How long since he'd held a woman close? Would he ever again?

'No!' Declan yanked his arm free, shoving her aside rather than feel the teasing brush of that rounded feminine form. 'I can do it myself. Just show me the way.' His other hand tightened around hers as frustration rose.

'Very well.'

Without another word she stepped forward, leading him. Declan put his weight on his good foot, and then supported himself on the ball of the injured one.

She didn't go too fast. Nor did she shilly shally and ask if he could keep up. It had taken him weeks to cure David of that and David was the best PA he'd ever had.

'There you are. The chair is to your left.' She took his left hand in hers and pulled him gently forward till he touched metal. 'There's the arm of it.'

She said no more but waited till he manoeuvred himself round and down into the seat.

'If you wait a few moments I'll go and get the first-aid kit.'

'I've got nowhere else to go.'

There was an almost inaudible huff of sound, as if he'd surprised a laugh out of her. Then she was gone and he was alone.

He should be used to it now, this sense of isolation. Sometimes it grew so intense it morphed into a crawling fear that one day he'd be left so completely alone in the dark he'd never be with others again. A childish terror, but one that still woke him in the middle of the night, chest heaving and heart pounding as he reached out, clawing at the inky darkness that enveloped him.

Declan reminded himself that solitude was what he'd always come to the mountains for. A change from the hectic pace of his overloaded schedule. His usually overloaded schedule.

No longer. He'd had to delegate more to keep up, despite David's assistance.

Anger, his ever-present companion, snarled in

his veins—till he reminded himself he'd been the lucky one.

Instantly the familiar fog of regret and guilt enveloped him. His stomach twisted. He should be thankful to have survived. Yet he couldn't convince himself it was for the best. His failure made this prison of blankness even more unbearable. If only he'd…

'Here you are. I've brought the first-aid supplies.' That voice again, cool and clear, yet with a richness that made him wonder what her singing voice was like.

'You had no trouble finding me, then?' Sarcasm was poor repayment for her assistance, but the caged beast that raged and growled inside demanded outlet. Declan's usual means of using up excess energy—skiing, climbing and sex—were denied him.

Sex was possible, he supposed. He'd have to get someone like this efficient housekeeper to find and dial the numbers in his private directory. For a moment he diverted himself, wondering how she'd react if he asked her to ring his ex-lovers. Would she sound so prim and proper then?

But he couldn't stomach the thought of sympathy sex. For that was what it would be.

Scorching anger churned in his belly. What woman would want him now?

He refused to be the object of anyone's pity, grateful for the crumbs they deigned to dole out now he was so much less than he'd been. Even the doctors played that game, holding out the possibility his sight might return, though never guaranteeing it.

'Your foot must be paining you after all.' He heard her put something on the paving stones.

'You know that for a fact, do you?' He'd got tired in hospital of the staff dictating what was best for him and how he should feel. Till he'd discharged himself early and come here to recuperate in private.

'I'm guessing. You're cranky, but I'm giving you the benefit of the doubt in thinking there's a reason for your tone.'

To his surprise, his mouth lifted in a twist of amusement that pulled unused muscles tight. He couldn't remember smiling since the accident.

'Where's your sympathy for the poor maimed invalid?'

'Probably the same place your manners are.' She paused and lifted his foot carefully to place it on something cushioned. A towel on her lap?

For some reason he rather enjoyed the idea of her kneeling at his feet.

'Besides,' she said as he felt gentle fingers touch his heel, 'You're not an invalid.'

Declan's mouth tightened and his hands curled into fists. Great, just great: another happy-clappy optimist. Just like the last rehab worker.

'What do you call this, then?' he jeered, jerking a hand in the direction of his glasses.

'Just because you can't see doesn't mean you're an invalid. The man I saw doing lap after lap in the pool was fitter and more agile than most people I know.' Her hold on his foot changed. 'This may hurt a little.'

It hurt a lot, but Declan was used to pain now. Getting walking again on that bad leg had taken more guts and determination than anything he'd ever done. It had been harder even than turning his back on family connections when he was a kid determined to build a business his own way.

'Most people can see what they're doing.' Was she deliberately obtuse?

'Are you looking for sympathy?'

'No!' Not that. Just…

Hell. He didn't know what he wanted. Just that he was tired of do-gooders telling him to look on the bright side.

'Good.' She pressed something to his heel. 'This is just to stop the blood. I don't think it needs stitches but I'd like the bleeding to slow before I dress it.'

'You're one tough cookie—is that it?' For the first time he wondered what sort of person his housekeeper was. What had made her so cool and capable in the face of a growling employer who wasn't fit company for anyone? 'Are you trying to prove yourself to me?'

'I'm simply trying to help so you don't get an infection in this foot.' Not even a hint of impatience in that controlled tone. For an unsettling moment Declan was reminded of his kindergarten teacher who'd had a way of quieting rambunctious little boys with just a look.

'What are you smiling at?'

'Was I smiling?' He firmed his mouth into its habitual line.

'This may hurt.'

Good. It might focus his straying mind.

Pain sliced through him as she applied antiseptic.

'What do you look like, Ms Daniels?'

For the first time she hesitated. *Intriguing.*

'Average,' she said firmly.

'On the tall side,' he amended.

'How do you know?'

Declan shrugged. 'The way you fitted under my arm.' He paused. 'What else?'

'Is this really necessary?'

'Indulge me. Think of it as the job interview I never gave you.'

'You're saying my job's in doubt?' For the first time a hint of emotion coloured her voice. Panic?

He shook his head. 'I'm not that unreasonable, just curious.'

He heard a huff of exasperation and then she was winding a bandage around his foot with deft movements that assured him she knew exactly what she was doing.

'I've got light hair, light eyes and pale skin.'

'Freckles?' Why he bothered to tease when he couldn't see her reaction he didn't know. But despite her calm responses Declan *felt* her disapproval. It shimmered around him. Tired as he was of his own company and his limitations, even that was preferable to solitude.

How pathetic could he get? Taunting the woman because he was bored, bitter and defeated by the guilt that clung like a shadow.

'Yes, as it happens. A few.' Her voice dropped a little and he caught a husky edge as she snapped shut the first-aid kit.

Declan surged to his feet. 'Thanks. Now, if

you'll just lead me to the edge of the pergola, I can find my way from there.'

Chloe stopped in the open doorway to the vast book-lined library. It had been updated with a state-of-the-art computer on the antique cedar desk and a phone that looked like it could hold conference calls to several countries simultaneously. Hand raised to knock, she paused at the sound of Declan Carstairs' voice.

'OK, David. There's no help for it, you'll just have to stay there. Don't worry about it.' Her employer thrust a hand back through his hair in a gesture of clear frustration. 'No, *don't* send one of the junior staff in the meantime. I don't want anyone here gawping and…' He hunched his shoulders. 'Never mind.'

He turned and she caught his expression. His face was drawn with weariness. Lines etched the corners of his mouth and furrowed his brow. Then she caught a glimpse of his eyes and wondered with a jolt if it was tiredness or something akin to despair that shadowed his face.

The notion surprised her. He'd seemed so vibrant, so arrogantly in control just half an hour ago. Even as he'd been dependent on her to lead him and remove the glass from his foot, there'd been no question but that he'd been the one calling the shots, and not just because he paid her wages. The force of his personality made him dominate any situation.

'No, I'll just have to wait till you—'

He broke off and lifted his head as if scenting the air, his head swinging round inexorably to where she stood in the doorway.

Dark eyes fixed on her with an intensity that was unnerving.

Even knowing he couldn't see her, Chloe had to resist the urge to straighten her neat skirt and blouse or lift a hand to ensure that flyaway curl hadn't escaped again. Heat trickled through her veins and her skin flushed.

'Call me later, David, and update me.' He disconnected the call and stepped towards her, his eyes never wavering.

Was it an illusion that his gaze connected with hers? It had to be. Yet Chloe felt a strange breathlessness facing that hard, handsome face, as if he saw her with a clarity no-one else ever had.

'Ms Daniels. How long have you been there?' His voice dropped to a velvet-soft murmur that signalled danger.

How did he know she was there? She hadn't

made a sound. The hairs rose on the back of her neck at the idea he'd somehow sensed her presence.

'Not long. I was about to knock but I didn't want to interrupt your conversation.'

His mouth firmed and his nostrils flared as if with impatience. 'In future make your presence known immediately. Given my…impairment, I like to know when I'm not alone.'

'Yes, sir.'

'Especially when I'm discussing business. I have a particularly delicate negotiation underway at the moment and I prefer to keep the details private. Understood?'

Chloe's mouth pursed, holding in indignation. Did he think her a potential corporate spy?

'Of course.' Stung at his assumption she'd tried to eavesdrop, Chloe hastened to explain herself. 'I came to find out if you'd like lunch soon.'

His mouth twisted. 'What have you got planned for me? No, let me guess—coddled eggs and toast. Or soup. Soup is always good.'

Chloe frowned, her mind racing through the contents of the pantry and what she could make quickly from scratch.

'If you like soup I could manage that.'

'I *don't* like,' he growled, pacing towards her, close enough to block her view of the room and fill her senses with his presence. 'I'm sick of bland food and being fussed over. The housekeeper the agency sent in your absence thought I needed cosseting to build my strength. If she'd had her way I'd have lived on omelettes and junket.' He shook his head, lifting a hand to rub his stubbled chin.

Unwillingly Chloe's eyes followed the movement, noting the hard, intriguing angle of his jaw and the line of his powerful throat. A faint citrus scent teased her nostrils and she wondered if he'd lathered himself with lemon soap in the shower. She swallowed. He hadn't buttoned his shirt. It hung loose, revealing glimpses of taut golden skin and a smattering of dark hair.

Her breath stilled as she recalled him emerging from the pool: naked, wet and virile. Her mouth dried.

Horrified to find her gaze following a narrow line of dark hair to the top of his faded jeans, Chloe yanked her attention back to his face, her cheeks glowing.

Anyone less in need of building up she had yet to meet. He was all hard-muscled energy and husky, powerful lines. She'd never met a man so vibrantly alive. So confrontingly masculine. Her stomach gave a strange little shimmy just being close to him.

'I hadn't thought in terms of…building up your strength.' Again her gaze strayed and she firmly yanked it back to his face.

Despite her embarrassment, amusement rose at the idea of trying to cosset this man like a child. The previous housekeeper must have had her work cut out trying to feed him invalid food. Had she *really* tried to serve him junket? Chloe wouldn't have dared.

'What was that?' His brows arrowed down ferociously as if he'd heard the laugh she stifled.

'Nothing, Mr Carstairs.' She paused. 'I'd planned chicken tikka-masala burgers with cucumber raita and lime pickle for lunch. But if that doesn't suit…'

'It suits perfectly. Suddenly I'm ravenous.' For a moment the shadow of a grin hovered on his lips and Chloe had a shocking glimpse of how irresistible he must be in good humour.

If ever he *was* in good humour.

'Clever too,' he drawled. 'Far easier for a blind man to handle.'

That observation, the little sting in the tail, robbed his earlier praise of warmth and left her deflated.

Was there anything wrong in trying to take his limitations into consideration? To realise it must be difficult chasing unseen food around a plate?

He made her consideration seem like condescension.

Her boss was frank to the point of rudeness, bad-tempered and graceless. He was nothing like his charmer of a brother.

A shiver whispered down her spine and she stiffened.

Chloe knew which brother she'd rather deal with. Declan Carstairs might be arrogant but...

'I'll have it ready in half an hour, then.'

'Good.' He turned away, took three uneven paces and put his hand down to the corner of the desk as if to reassure himself he was in the right place. It was a subtle move she wouldn't have noticed except that her brain was busy cataloguing everything about him.

Instantly she felt a pang of sympathy. How hard it must be for an active man to adjust to a world he couldn't see.

Perhaps his temper was understandable.

'Before you go, Ms Daniels.' She paused in the act of turning away. 'Tell me, you did sign a confidentiality clause with your contract of employment, didn't you?'

'I did.'

'Then you know the severe penalties for revealing private information about anything you see or hear in the course of your work.'

Chloe drew a deep breath, telling herself he was within his rights to check, just as he'd been to insist she sign such a clause before working for him. It had nothing to do with her personal integrity.

'I understand that.' Nevertheless her fingers curled tight.

'Good. Keep it in mind. Because I'd have no hesitation in suing an employee who betrayed my trust if, for instance details of this current deal, or personal information about my life, were to appear in the press.'

Chloe's hackles rose. Did he distrust all his employees on principle or just her?

That fragile stirring of sympathy withered, replaced by a belligerent determination to keep out of Declan Carstairs' way. She didn't need to listen to his provocation. She had enough on her plate with worry about Ted's health and meeting the cost of his rehabilitation.

'I've worked for celebrities in the past, Mr Carstairs. People hounded by the paparazzi every time they stepped outside.' Her tone, more frigid than cool, implied they were far more newsworthy than he, despite the fact he was one of the country's richest men. 'None of them ever had complaints about my discretion.'

'Really?' One dark eyebrow arched provocatively.

'Really. Now, if you'll excuse me, Mr Carstairs, I'll get on with lunch.'

Chloe immersed herself in the routine of keeping the house in tip-top condition. A magnificent sprawling place, it dated from the nineteenth century. Her favourite feature was the wide veranda with its vista of manicured gardens. The gardens led to the cliff edge that dropped sheer to the blue-green valley, which spread into the distance.

Built at a time when a rich man included a ballroom in his country retreat, the place was a pleasure to work in. Especially as a wing had been added with a modern kitchen and housekeeper's suite.

She loved the gracious old home and didn't mind that it took a lot to maintain. That gave her reason to avoid the corner study where Declan Carstairs spent his time.

Occasionally as she crossed the lobby she heard his rich baritone on the phone or chatting to his PA, David Sarkesian, who'd returned from Sydney. The sound of her employer's deep voice made her quicken her pace lest he accuse her of eavesdropping for saleable gossip.

That insinuation still burned.

As did the suspicion that she enjoyed listening to the smooth rhythms of his voice for too much. The tingling awareness she felt in Declan Carstairs' presence disturbed her. It reminded her that, contrary to everything she'd learned in the last six years, her libido hadn't died with Mark.

She wished it had. She didn't need that hot, edgy sensation low in her stomach when Declan touched her hand reaching for a plate. Or the breathless anticipation that caught her lungs when he spoke to her.

She even enjoyed the verbal wrangling that seemed to be part of daily life working for him. He never let an encounter go by without challenging, probing or teasing till she almost suspected he looked forward to provoking her responses.

At least it prevented her dwelling on memories of the last time she'd lived here, when her dream job had turned into a nightmare.

'It's over now. You need to put it behind you,' she told her reflection in the bathroom mirror.

Easier said than done when fragmented nightmares still shattered her dreams. That was why she'd forced herself to come in here, to what had been Adrian Carstairs' suite.

Better to face the past squarely.

She'd learned that when she lost Mark years ago. The shock of grief, the unfairness of it, had kept her in denial for ages, trying to cling to a life that was past. It was only when she accepted the devastating blow that had stolen their dreams that she was able to move on.

Chloe swiped a cloth over the vanity unit.

'The past is gone.'

When she lost Mark those words had been a lament. Now there was relief that the trauma of Adrian Carstairs' frightening obsession was over. No matter how much she regretted his death, she couldn't help feeling a sense of freedom that he'd never stalk her again. That his dangerous fixation was over.

She picked up her cleaning supplies and turned, only to walk into a wall of naked male muscle.

She was soft, lithe and warm as his arms instinctively closed around her. The unexpectedness of contact momentarily stunned Declan, but a second later his body was responding to the intimate contact.

Predictable, he supposed, since he hadn't had a lover since well before the accident.

Yet why did his grip tighten when she moved to pull away? Surely not because he enjoyed the feel of her slender hand splayed across his bare chest? The gentle, almost phantom caress of her breath near his collarbone?

'Ms Daniels, I presume?' He forced himself into speech, covering his abrupt loss of control.

'Mr Carstairs, I didn't expect to see you here.'

There was a slightly breathless quality to her usually crisp voice as if he'd caught her out in some way.

He liked it.

Just as he liked the firm yet enticingly soft curves pressed against him.

This was Chloe Daniels, his sharp-tongued, no-nonsense housekeeper? She sounded young, but he'd supposed her voice was misleading. She was nothing like those sturdy, slightly frumpish women who'd staffed the various Carstairs properties in his childhood.

This woman was slim but curved in all the right places. 'Luscious' was the word that sprang to mind. His fingers tightened.

A familiar surge of frustration hit him: impatience that he couldn't see her for himself. Anger at this disability. Damn his blindness! Would he ever be whole again? He'd been curious about her so long and now, holding her, he had more questions than ever.

'I didn't expect to find you here either. I thought I heard voices.'

No need to say the muffled sound of conversation from Adrian's room had hit him like a sledgehammer blow to the heart. He'd dropped the shirt he'd taken off as he reached the head of the stairs and hurried here, nerves strung tight.

He wasn't a fanciful man but to his guilt-ridden conscience, the sound of talking from Adrian's suite had seemed portentous.

'I was talking to myself.' She sounded defiant rather than defensive, as if challenging him to make an issue of it. He was intrigued at this facet of his ever-practical employee.

'Indeed?'

'I'm sorry I disturbed you. I was just doing a quick clean.'

'No one will be using the suite.' He'd lost his taste for company the day he'd lost his brother.

'I understand.' She paused then added, her voice low, 'I'm sorry about your brother, Mr Carstairs.'

'Thank you,' he said tersely, dropping his hands.

Familiar guilt swamped him—that he was here,

alive, experiencing a surge of sexual interest for this woman, when Adrian was dead. He'd failed his younger brother.

He should have been able to stop him.

His stomach lurched sickeningly. They'd been close, despite their recent geographical separation. He'd been Adrian's biggest supporter, the one Adrian had turned to when their parents had been busy with their business and charity interests.

But that counted for nothing. All that mattered was that last, irrevocable failure.

How had he let himself be persuaded by Adrian's upbeat assurances? He should have come here sooner, not relied on phone and email during that vital phase of his new project. How could he not have *known* Adrian was in such despair?

'Is there anything else, Mr Carstairs?'

Declan plunged a hand through his shaggy hair. He wished there was something else—something to distract him.

Work was no solace. It couldn't ease the weight of remorse.

Nor could the search for the woman who'd used his little brother then tossed him aside when she found he'd lost his wealth. Her betrayal had driven Adrian to suicide. Any doubts Declan had about her guilt had been obliterated by the scrawled note

David had found jammed in Declan's desk. As soon as he'd recognised Adrian's handwriting he'd told Declan, who'd insisted he read it aloud.

Neither had spoken of it since but the words were engraved in Declan's memory: desperate words that confirmed Adrian's unnamed girlfriend, the woman he'd been seeing those last weeks, had pushed him to the edge.

Yet the private investigator had turned up no clue to her identity. Where had she vanished to?

Declan's mouth tightened. Adrian had always been the more sensitive one and, he realised now, more vulnerable. Declan felt impotent, unable to find the woman who'd destroyed his brother and make her face what she'd done.

He gulped down bitter regret, concentrating instead on the burning hate that sustained him when the burden of guilt grew unbearable.

Self-hatred for not saving his brother.

Hatred too for the woman with red-gold hair and come-hither green eyes in the photo his brother had shown him so proudly. A photo so candid it was obvious he'd taken the shot in bed. The woman had lain sprawled in abandon, as if sated from love-making. Golden light had bathed her, giving her the aura of a languid sex goddess inviting adoration.

And Declan had felt a shot of pure, unadulterated lust blast through him at the sight of her.

Remembering made him sick to the stomach, as if he'd betrayed his brother with his response to the woman Adrian had loved. The woman who'd driven Adrian to fatal despair.

Between them they were responsible for Adrian's death.

CHAPTER THREE

HE NO longer touched her, yet Chloe burned as if still pressed against him.

Shivers trembled down her spine. She had to lock her knees to stand firm. But nothing, not all her willpower, could prevent her dragging in the scent of citrus and man, spice and warm musk, that tickled her nostrils. Her gaze strayed to his half-naked form.

She'd never seen anyone like Declan Carstairs— his powerful, beautiful body and his larger-than-life aura. Unshaven, hard-jawed and scarred he looked more then ever like a pirate. The sort who thrived on danger and the pleasures of the flesh.

Chloe tried to recall Mark's generous smile, the twinkle of encouragement in his hazel eyes and, to her horror, conjured only the weakest of images. Could she have forgotten in just six years? Or was Declan Carstairs clouding her thoughts? The idea appalled her.

Eyes wide, she retreated a step and put down her bucket of supplies, crossing her arms defensively.

'Mr Carstairs? If there's nothing else I really should be getting on.'

A flicker of movement stirred his features as if he'd only just recalled her presence. Why did he look so grim?

'Actually there is something, Ms Daniels.'

He flexed his hands, drawing her gaze to the sinewy strength in his forearms.

What would it be like to be held by him? Not supported impersonally after bumping into each other, but embraced?

It felt like betrayal of her past even to wonder. Yet she couldn't prevent the niggle of curiosity.

'You were working here when my brother came to stay, weren't you? While I was in China?'

Instantly alert, Chloe darted a look at his face.

'Yes. I'd been here some time when he arrived.' Anxiety jiggled inside. Just the mention of Adrian Carstairs gave her the jitters.

How could one brother fascinate and reawaken long-dormant female awareness when the other had left her cold?

'Tell me, did he bring anyone to stay with him?'

She shook her head, remembering too late that

Declan needed to hear her response. 'No, he came alone.'

'But there must have been visitors.' Dark eyes fixed at a point near her mouth, as if focused on her words. She sensed an intensity in her employer she hadn't encountered before, even when he'd quizzed her about confidentiality.

'There were no overnight guests.'

'But for a meal perhaps?'

'No, not that I recall. Your brother ate alone.'

Except for the days he'd turned up in the big kitchen and insisted on sharing a meal with her.

At first Chloe had welcomed him. Then, when he had grown more intense—his gaze fixing on her hungrily, his moods unstable—she'd taken to eating early in her room or finding an excuse to be away at meal time.

But she couldn't say that to his brother. There was nothing to be gained by sharing the fact Adrian Carstairs had made her life hell those last weeks. Declan had enough to deal with without her dumping that on him.

'I see.' Yet still he frowned, his brows bunched. 'But it's possible he had a visitor you didn't know about?'

'It's possible,' she said slowly. 'Though not likely.'

Increasingly Adrian had spent his time within

sight of her until she'd had to resort to subterfuge to escape him. She'd have been grateful then for visitors to distract him from his fixation on her.

'He didn't mention anyone?' The urgency of her boss's tone surprised her.

'I… Not that I recall.'

'I see.' Declan's head sank slowly, as if weighted. The vibrant energy that was so much part of him dimmed and she sensed despair.

Impulsively she lifted her hand to him, then let it drop. She could imagine his sharp rejection of unwanted sympathy.

'I'm sorry I can't help.'

His lips curved in a twist that might have passed for a smile if it weren't for the grim lines creasing his cheek and pulling his scar tight.

'No matter.' He lifted a hand to thrust back a lock of dark hair from his brow. 'But if you recall seeing a woman with gold hair—a friend of Adrian's—you'll let me know? I'm trying to contact her. It's…important.'

'Of course.'

Chloe frowned. Adrian had never mentioned a girlfriend. He'd seemed a loner.

'Good.' For a moment longer Declan stood, as if wanting to prolong conversation. Then he turned and paced stiffly away, arm out in front of him till he reached the hall door and disappeared towards his room.

'I have a favour to ask.'

Chloe spun round to find her employer leaning against the doorjamb as if he'd been there for ages, watching her.

Her pulse accelerated. Though he clearly hadn't been watching, she was unsettled by the notion he'd been there, listening to her potter in the kitchen, humming under her breath.

Yet even as the thought surfaced, she realised it wasn't anxiety she felt. Not like when his brother had stalked her, silently watching with an intensity that had given her the creeps.

No, this was different—a spiralling drop of excitement that drew her skin tight and clenched her stomach muscles in awareness. It had everything to do with her inability to blot Declan Carstairs from her brain.

His charismatic presence had banished the last shadows of anxiety she'd felt about returning to Carinya.

At least now her dreams weren't all nightmares, she admitted with a grimace. The last few nights she'd woken hot and shaken by vivid fantasies fea-

turing Declan in glorious, nude detail. An insidi-
ous little tremor shot through her at the memory.

'Yes, Mr Carstairs?' She injected her tone with
a brisk efficiency she was far from feeling.

He straightened and stepped into the room, turning to the sound of her voice.

'I have a meeting in Sydney and I want to be rid
of this beard.' He lifted one hand ruminatively to
his chin and Chloe heard the scratch of bristles.

For one insane moment she was tempted to lift
her hand so they rasped against her palm. She
could almost feel the rough pleasure of that tickle
on her skin.

The realisation hit her like a hammer blow, rob-
bing her of speech.

How had she grown so desperate for this man?
Just imagining the scrape of his unshaven skin
made her insides liquefy. How could that be? They
weren't friends or anything like lovers. She barely
knew him! With Mark, desire had grown with lik-
ing, with love. By comparison this was a smash-
and-grab raid on her senses.

'David's gone on ahead so I wondered if you'd
oblige. I can just about get by with an electric razor
but it's pretty haphazard.'

'Of course, Mr Carstairs. I'm happy to help. But
I should warn you, I've never shaved anyone.'

'Then I'll be your first.' His mouth widened in a slow smile that snagged her heart mid-beat. 'A first for us both.'

Not once in these last weeks had he smiled at her properly. Chloe wished fervently he hadn't decided to begin. She sagged against the worktop, her hand to the pulse trembling in her throat. Just as well he couldn't see her.

Even blind and scarred the man was devastating. What would he be like if he set his mind to seducing a woman?

She should be grateful for his usually brusque manner. It was a buffer to what she guessed could be formidable charm. His rare smile set her heart hammering.

'Shall we say my bathroom in five?'

Though she'd lived with Mark for almost a year, Chloe hadn't realised how intimate shaving a man could be.

Standing between Declan's splayed knees as he sat on the bathroom stool, jammed between the basin on her right and the wall at her back, she felt hemmed in. Not by the room, but by his proximity.

Her breathing shallowed as she slid the razor over his foamy cheek, too aware of the soft puff of his breath against her shirt and the heat of his legs around hers.

Her hand trembled and slowed.

'Like this.' His hand closed on hers, guiding her. She tried to concentrate on the shape of his jaw, the need to be careful. Yet her mind kept straying to the way his long fingers encircled hers.

'Got it?' His hand dropped and she sucked in a breath.

'I think so.' She cleaned the blade then made herself lean in, stoically ignoring his citrus scent and concentrating on the next stroke of the blade.

He sat statue-still and she told herself this would get easier. Except she made the mistake of looking into his eyes between strokes, intrigued to find they weren't blank as expected. Even unseeing they fascinated her. Deepest brown, so dark they hinted at blackness, yet rayed at the centre with a rim of golden shards.

'Chloe?' The question in his voice focused her wandering thoughts.

'Yes, Mr Carstairs?' This time she dared to tilt his chin for better access, telling herself the faster she got this done the sooner he'd leave and she'd be alone, safe from these unsettling feelings.

'Just checking,' he murmured. 'Given the circumstances, you can drop the "Mr Carstairs". It sounds too formal when you're holding a razor to my throat.'

Chloe rinsed off the razor and tilted his head further to the side, trying to ignore the fact his face was bare inches from her breasts. And that her nipples puckered flagrantly against the lace of her bra.

'You *are* my employer,' she protested, clinging to formality to counter the rising tide of utterly inappropriate feelings. She looked down, registering the way his jeans clung to solid, muscled thighs and felt a jab of longing deep in her belly.

'So, if I don't mind you calling me Declan, there's no reason to refuse.'

Silently she shook her head and ventured another stroke down the hard line of his cheek. The scrape of the blade against his skin was curiously sensuous. There was something intriguing about revealing the strong contours of his face with each careful stroke.

'Do it, Chloe.' The words feathered the bare flesh above the top button of her shirt and a line of tingling fire ran from her tight breasts to her groin.

'Sorry?'

'Say my name.'

'I really don't think…' It was stupid to refuse, but at some instinctive level she knew she'd be crossing into dangerous territory from which there'd be no retreat.

'Are you contradicting me?' His deep voice slid like silk across her skin.

'Are you ordering me?'

She watched his mouth lift at one corner.

'How did you get this job when you're so unwilling to comply with reasonable requests?'

It was on the tip of her tongue to say that calling him Declan wasn't reasonable. That it might reveal the pent-up longing she'd been trying so hard to repress, the very unprofessional thoughts she'd been able to hide only because he couldn't see.

'If that's what you want,' she said grudgingly.

'I want.'

His eyes lowered. Did he realise he appeared to be looking straight at her breasts? Was that why a smile flickered at the corner of his mouth? She made to step back, only to find his thighs imprisoned her. A pulse of sensation throbbed low in her body.

'As you wish.'

'Out loud, Chloe.'

She drew a deep breath, telling herself she was making a mountain out of a molehill.

'Declan.'

There. It was done. The word was easy and she sounded confident.

So why did she lick her lips as if she'd just tasted a forbidden delicacy? Why the jitter of excitement at the echo of his name on her tongue?

'Good. Now, stop delaying. I know it must look appalling but it's just dead skin.'

For a moment Chloe stared, uncomprehending. Then finally she realised. His scar. She'd stopped before shaving there. He thought she was wary of touching it.

Carefully she rinsed the razor.

'It doesn't look appalling.' The words emerged, a hoarse whisper, before she knew they'd even formulated in her mind.

'Don't give me that!' The lingering trace of amusement died and his lips thinned in a cruel, hard line. 'I don't need lies to keep me sweet. I know I look like the very devil.'

'No.' The choked protest welled from her.

That long, mobile mouth twisted in a sneer. 'No?' His nostrils flared as he dragged in a breath that pumped his whole torso. 'Then what, pray tell, does it look like?' Cynicism skeined through his words like silk.

The venom, the strength of his anger, was a vibrant, living force, pulsing from him in waves.

Instinctively Chloe stepped back, or tried to. His thighs, iron-hard and unmoveable, trapped her. Something hot twisted low in her belly.

'Come on, Chloe,' he taunted. 'I deserve to know.'

Her mouth flattened at his baiting tone, even as she realised his fury stemmed from issues that had nothing to do with her. That he was still coming to grips with the legacy of the accident that had blinded him.

'I didn't say it's beautiful.'

'Ah, at last, something like the truth!'

Her hands fisted as she stared down into his grim face. 'But it's not as bad as you think. It gives you…character.'

No way could she be frank enough to add that the way it followed the natural line of his cheek complemented his strong features. Or that she'd come to appreciate the asymmetrical cast of his face that saved it from being too dauntingly perfect.

It made him look dangerous and sexy and far too intriguing.

'Character!' A jeering laugh burst from his lips. 'That's a good one.'

'It's true.' The fire inside, the heat of unwanted

arousal, twisted and morphed into a dangerous mix of distress and anger.

He shook his head, his hands clamping on his thighs as if to restrain himself from pushing her aside and shooting to his feet.

'I do not need your sympathy.' Each glacial word dropped with the pinpoint accuracy of a precision bomb, designed with lethal intent.

A shiver sped up Chloe's spine and her skin iced. She hunched her shoulders.

'No, but you need to stop feeling so sorry for yourself.'

The words burst into echoing silence.

The razor clattered, unheeded, into the sink and Chloe found herself standing, arms akimbo, staring furiously down into eyes that darkened to ebony. A pulse jumped at his temple and the air throbbed with a surge of dangerous power.

Silence stretched till her nerves were taut with expectation. She couldn't believe she'd answered back that way. He was her boss. The man who paid her wages.

Yet she cared about him. Cared enough, it seemed, to risk the sack to tell him the truth.

The unnerving realisation froze her while the ramifications played out in her mind.

Abruptly he raised his hand, fumbling in front

of him till long fingers touched her hip. She told herself she imagined the imprint burning through her skirt. But she didn't imagine the burst of heat when his fingers found hers, locking them hard and tight in his hold.

He yanked her hand to his face, to the point beside his eye where the scar ended.

A tremor hit her as he pressed her finger on the damaged flesh so she felt the ridge of healed tissue. But her overwhelming impression was of heat and excitement—an illicit thrill that skirled in her abdomen, clenching muscles.

Slowly, oh so slowly, he dragged her hand down, her fingers to the scar, her hand dwarfed by his.

Through the shaving cream, centimetre by centimetre the skin-to-skin contact continued. It was a punishment, a challenge, yet to Chloe it had the force of a caress. Potent, provocative, drawing out hidden longings and exposing them, raw and unvarnished, to the light of day.

His warm skin scent was inside her; his heat infused hers. The prison of his long legs evoked a delicious, terrible thrill she fought and failed to conquer.

Now her hand was beside his mouth, pressed there, feeling the supple skin stretch as he spoke.

'You have the gall to call that *character*?'

She opened her mouth but before she could speak he dragged her hand away. A blob of shaving cream fell from their joined fingers.

Did he know he held her so tight that the sensation bordered on pain?

'Or this?' He slammed her hand, palm down on his thigh, right up near his hip.

Chloe's heart galloped high in her chest as she looked at her fingers splayed under his, moulding the wide muscle of his upper leg. Her breath came in raw, shallow gasps at the intensity of the contact.

At his fury. His frustration. Her regret, sorrow and still, through it all, the unrepentant hum of sexual energy that furred her nape and drew her breasts tight and full and heavy.

Under his guidance her hand slid down over soft denim that covered hot flesh and uneven scar-tissue.

The wound was long and jagged.

'What would you call that, Chloe?' The jeering note had faded from his voice, replaced by a weariness that betrayed the effort it took to face the world as if it was his for the taking.

These last weeks she'd marvelled at his confidence, his ability to adapt within mere months to his life-changing injuries. His ability to stride without pause through the open French windows of the study, unerringly cross the flagstones and dive without hesitation into the pool. To run a multinational company despite his impairment.

He even had time to parry and riposte verbally whenever their paths crossed, as if drawing her into conflict was a challenge that afforded him pleasure.

Now, feeling the tremors running through his thigh, the fierce clench of his hand, she glimpsed a fraction of what it cost him to appear in control.

Her heart missed a beat as another protective layer crumbled. Soon there'd be nothing left to keep her safe.

'Well, Chloe?' His voice dropped low, reverberating right through her. 'Is that full of character too? Should I be *grateful* for the accident that blinded me?'

'Maybe it sounds trite, but there are lots of people worse off than you.' Chloe drew a slow breath, refusing to be cowed by his anger. 'You have your health. You're mobile. You have the satisfaction of running your own business. You have enough money to live in comfort. Millions of others aren't that lucky.'

She spoke from experience. Her own foster father, Ted, had been an active, energetic man whom nothing could daunt. Now, still grieving the loss of his wife, he was confined to a rehabilitation clinic, recuperating slowly from the stroke that had immobilised one side of his body and robbed him of speech. And then there was Mark. His death at twenty-two had been fate at its cruellest.

'You're right,' he snapped. 'It does sound trite.'

'I'm sorry.' Not for speaking the truth, but that he obviously wasn't ready to hear it.

His sightless eyes glittered with barely leashed emotion.

'Do you have any idea how infuriating it is to be lectured about looking on the bright side? About how *lucky* I am? To have false hope of recovery held out like a holy grail?'

'No.' She stood stiffly.

'No.' His expression was grim. 'How could you know?'

Abruptly he stood, making her shuffle a half-step into the corner to give him room. Still, he held her hand and she wondered if he'd forgotten it.

But then, with a sudden, unerring accuracy, he lifted their joined hands to her cheek. Together they stroked the contour of her cheekbone and her skin came alive at the incredible intimacy of their joined touch.

'You're whole,' he said, so low it was like a vibration rather than a sound. 'Your life hasn't turned upside down so that everything you took for granted—*everything*—is now exponentially more difficult if not downright impossible.'

Their hands traced down to the corner of her mouth and a ripple of awareness shook her.

'You're not dogged by regret over what you *couldn't* do, that you failed the one person who above all relied on you.'

He was talking about Adrian, she realised, and her heart squeezed. She wanted to tell him she knew the guilt that came with loss. She'd spent so long bedevilled by guilt because she hadn't recognised the signs of meningitis early enough to save Mark.

But it was too soon for Declan to listen to reason. His fury was too fresh, too raw.

Perhaps she shouldn't have stood up to him. He was still coming to grips with his changed lifestyle and his loss.

Suddenly he loosened his hold and let her hand fall. It tingled as blood rushed back.

Yet he didn't move away. His tall frame crowded her into the corner, making her acutely aware of how her wayward body responded to him. Even tipping her head up to look into his face shot a tiny thrill through her.

He was her employer. Feelings of this sort were totally inappropriate.

That didn't stop anticipation swirling through her.

His hand settled on her face, fingers spreading to mould her jaw.

Chloe sucked in a startled breath as he slid his hand over her, cupping her chin and circling her cheek almost as if he could picture her face through touch.

Each stroke reinforced the urgent, eager need for more. It was all she could do to stand still, not tilt her head into his hand.

Her response scared her.

With Mark there'd been fun, shared joy, respect. She couldn't remember anything like the visceral urgency she felt when Declan Carstairs merely brushed his hand over her skin in the questing gesture of a blind man.

'How old are you, Chloe Daniels?' His voice hit that low, rich note that made something curl inside her.

'Twenty-seven.' She straightened and tilted her chin higher, only to find his hand dropping to her throat as if she'd invited his feather-light caress there.

Had she?

Whorls of lazy heat eddied at his touch and her head eased back.

She gulped, desperately trying to regain her composure. 'How old are you?'

Long fingers stroked her lips, cajoling her into silence.

'Thirty-four.' His head tipped towards her as if, even blind, it was important that he look her in the eyes.

'Thirty-four, blind and scarred. Not the man I was.'

His voice was an indictment, as if he saw himself as less a man than before.

He leaned towards her and her breath caught.

'And you, Chloe, are smooth and young and unscarred.' He paused while his hand traced her nose and returned with heart-stopping intent to her mouth. Her lips felt swollen and pulsing, as if waiting for more than the touch of his hand.

Fire sparked in her veins and she found herself straining towards him.

'You're whole,' he murmured. 'And I'm...'

He shook his head, his mouth grim, even as he framed her face with his fingers, letting them slide through her hair. Tremulous delight filled her at his gentle massaging pressure.

Then, with an abruptness that floored her, his

hands dropped and he stepped back, his shoulders stiff, his face a forbidding mask not even the smear of shaving cream could humanise.

'I don't want you here.'

The statement, so simple, so unambiguous, stuck in her dazed mind as if he spoke in a foreign tongue.

When she didn't move, his brow pleated in a ferocious scowl. His hands curled into tight fists.

'Get out of here, Chloe.' Words spat from him like bullets. 'Now!'

CHAPTER FOUR

DECLAN paced the empty boardroom his staff had scurried to leave. The pace of the China project was too slow and he hadn't minced his words.

He felt so bloody powerless, managing from a distance. Unable to see the figures for himself, view the footage of the site, read the faces of the consortium partners during the video hook-up.

He spun on his foot and strode down the room, registering the faint heat from the long windows beside him. They gave a spectacular view over the Domain and the no-doubt sparkling waters of Sydney Harbour, right to the Heads where the sea swell surged in from the Pacific.

A multi-million-dollar view he'd never see again despite the doctors' talk of possible recovery. They said there was no lasting physical damage to keep him blind.

As if he *chose* not to see!

He shoved back the hair flopping over his forehead and turned to pace. At least with the room's simple layout he wasn't going to trip over furniture and make himself a laughing stock.

Maybe he should be grateful for *that* too.

Chloe's words rang in his head—that there were people worse off than himself.

Did she think he didn't know that? There was barely a minute ticked by when he wasn't acutely aware that Adrian was dead, not merely maimed and blind.

Or that Declan was the one who'd failed to save him.

How dared she accuse him of feeling sorry for himself?

Who was she to lecture him? To talk in platitudes about something she didn't understand?

She was young, too young surely for the responsible job of running Carinya. Her skin still had the smooth, taut texture of youth. Unblemished and perfect.

Declan clenched his fists, recalling the pulse of need that had shot through him as he'd traced her features, learnt the high curve of cheekbones and delicate point of her chin. Her silk-soft hair, pulled back from her face. Her neat nose and soft, plump lips.

Damn! His fist pounded the toughened glass

window with a dull thud that did nothing to ease the turbulent roil of emotions churning his gut.

Anger—yes.

Impatience—that was a given.

Frustration—that word had taken on a whole new meaning since Chloe Daniels had entered his home. Before that he'd been frustrated merely with his blindness, his incompetence in this world of darkness, his inability to find and punish the callous woman who'd driven Adrian to his death. That failure ate like a canker at his soul.

Now Declan's frustration had the keen edge of sexual hunger. The ever-present hint of Chloe's vanilla-sunshine scent in his home tantalised his nostrils and fed the gnawing hunger in his belly.

For too long his dreams had been haunted by Adrian's fall. Now they'd changed, waking him nightly, sweating and with his heart pounding.

He could barely make himself face it but those dreams featured not just Adrian, but the woman in his brother's treasured photo—the lover who'd betrayed him. Yet, instead of hatred, it was lust that sizzled through Declan as he dreamed of her, sprawled and voluptuous.

His fist pounded futilely on the glass and he hung his head, shame washing him.

Bad enough to feel that instantaneous spark of

interest when Ade had shown him the photo. Far worse to dream of her and imagine she had Chloe's clear voice, her quick mind, her impossibly soft skin.

It was as if he betrayed both his brother and the woman he employed. The woman who'd done nothing wrong but stand up to him rather than kowtow like most of his staff. Who'd unwittingly provided comfort and company with her gentle presence when he most needed it.

She sparked a sense of life and energy in him with her independent, almost combative attitude. She drew him back from the dark maw of despair that hovered close. He'd even taken to finding excuses to seek her out.

Until the day he'd left Carinya.

He'd been within a breath of grabbing her, had been perilously close to losing control. If she hadn't left at his command, he'd have had her hard and fast against the bathroom wall. His groin throbbed just remembering that dangerously charged atmosphere, the way her voice had turned husky as his blood had thrummed with desire. He'd wanted her with a desperation that scared him. A desperation that would have terrified his prim and proper Ms Daniels if she'd known.

With an oath he turned and strode to the door. He

needed to find David and get to work. Anything to stop thinking too much.

Halfway to the door he collided with a chair that hadn't been pushed back to the conference table. His momentum hurtled him forward. When he grabbed the chair it slid sideways. He tumbled to the carpet, his bad knee a sear of burning pain and his dignity in tatters.

He lay there, winded.

A bitter laugh escaped.

Back at Carinya he'd allowed himself to fantasise that Chloe had felt that quake of connection too: the heart-in-mouth desire that turned him weak at the feel of her body heat or the hint of her vanilla-and-woman scent in his nostrils.

He was a fool.

What woman would want him like this?

'Mr Carstairs?' Chloe prided herself on her cool, professional voice as she paused at the study door. Yet her pulse beat faster at the prospect of seeing him.

Declan had been like a bear with a sore head since his Sydney trip. She hoped it was because of business problems instead of that scene in his bathroom—the day she'd almost flung her arms around his neck and kissed his cynical, sensuous mouth with all the passion building inside her.

She shivered at how close she'd come to making herself a laughing stock. She could imagine the poised, beautiful women Declan spent time with. Even blind he wouldn't want a housekeeper with practical shoes and work-roughened hands.

It stunned her that she wanted him to notice her. As if she liked living on a knife-edge of excitement.

'Yes?' His tone was brusque, reinforcing his status as tycoon employer and hers as paid underling.

It was the reminder she needed. She and her employer had nothing in common except their address. And yet...

'I just took a call from David... Mr Sarkesian.' She glanced across to the desk where the phone was off the hook. Was his mobile switched off too? Lately Declan spent too much time brooding, or so it seemed to her.

It bothered her that she cared quite as much as she did. Enough to want to comfort him.

He wouldn't appreciate that.

'I know who he is.' It was an impatient growl, as if she'd interrupted him in the middle of important work. Yet he'd been staring sightlessly towards the window.

She tried to ignore her heart's abrupt lurch of sympathy. Despite his wealth and power, he was so very much alone. Declan shunned the possibility of anyone supporting him through his grief and recuperation.

Chloe stepped further into the room, refusing to shout across the vast space. Unerringly his head turned towards her as if he could pinpoint her exact location even after she crossed from the polished floor to the heirloom carpet.

The uncanny movement made her falter. Despite logic, despite all the rules, there *was* more between them than boss and servant.

She'd only ever been intimate with Mark, the man she'd married. Yet her connection with Declan felt intimate in ways she didn't understand.

'Well?'

She thinned her lips, refusing to respond to his terse tone. 'It's bad news, I'm afraid. David has just been to the doctor. He's got chickenpox.'

'You're kidding! He's thirty. Only kids get chickenpox.'

She shrugged. 'Apparently it can be more severe in adults. He didn't sound well. The doctor advised he'd be off work for a couple of weeks.'

'A couple of weeks?' Declan's expression froze.

'He asked if you wanted one of the junior staff

to come and help with the current projects and any other matters…' Her voice trailed off. David was Declan's guide, the pair of eyes he no longer had. Those 'other matters' involved helping Declan with day-to-day tasks when he grew impatient with his own efforts.

Declan's face turned stony. Instantly she recalled his expression when she'd shaved him. Heat burst out of nowhere and coiling tension swirled deep inside, undermining her effort to remain professional.

How could she go on like this?

'I'll call him myself.' Declan sounded subdued, not like the arrogantly assured man who drove her crazy with his strong opinions and certainty he was right.

She opened her mouth to offer to dial the number then stopped. The merest whiff of sympathy was anathema to him.

'Then I'll get back to my duties.'

'Not so quickly.'

'Yes, Mr Carstairs?'

His lips thinned. 'Declan, remember?'

Oh, she remembered all right. Remembered so well her nipples tugged into hard peaks just thinking of that scene in his bathroom. His proximity, the touch of his skin, had fed a shocking hunger that time hadn't assuaged.

'Is there anything else I can do for you?' Chloe focused on his evident displeasure that she hadn't used his name. It was better than letting her mind stray to the things she'd like to do for him.

Heat suffused her skin. She couldn't remember ever feeling so overwhelmed, so wanton. Selfishly, she was glad he couldn't read her face. One look and he'd know her weakness for him. Sex, she told herself. That was all it was. Physical attraction. All she had to do was keep out of his way and eventually it would fade.

'Come back in an hour. I need someone to check my emails. Normally David would read them to me, but now...' He shrugged and spread his arms. Chloe read diffidence in the set of his shoulders but sensed it was camouflage. There was no mistaking the impatience behind his mask of calm.

It must gall him to be dependent on anyone.

'Until a replacement for David arrives?' Surely she could manage a few hours working with Declan.

He shook his head. 'There'll be no replacement. David knows my ways and so do you.' For one long moment it seemed he was looking at her, delving into those cravings she tried hard to hide. Inevitably, reaction stirred.

'You and I can work together until David returns. I don't need anyone else.'

Her heart dived.

In other words he didn't want anyone else to see him vulnerable, at a disadvantage because of his blindness. *She* didn't matter. She'd already seen him furious when he spilled food down his shirt or mislaid something.

She shivered, disturbed to realise she wanted him to want her for herself, not to shore up his pride.

More importantly she knew working with him daily would be a disaster—like walking a knife-edge. She'd never cope.

'What you mean is you're afraid to have anyone else here.'

Declan's head shot round, following the sound of her voice as she moved closer.

'What did you say?'

Was he hearing things now?

'You're scared of someone else seeing you vul-nerable.'

She stopped before him. Her voice was low and close. Her light scent swirled around him.

Furious as much at his awareness of her as at her

words, he lifted a hand to grab her, then stopped at the last moment. Remember what happened last time he'd touched her? How compelling the need to take more? To take *her*, with all the pent-up desperation of a blind man groping for the light? He'd never before been so needy. Or so bereft.

His arm dropped as if weighted with lead. Fire scorched his skin—desire and guilt. And fury.

'I don't employ you to pass judgment on my actions. I employ you to do what I say.'

'Even when it's a mistake?' Was that a wobble in her voice? As if she was nervous. She should be!

'I decide what's right for my business. No one questions my judgement.'

'You're saying you want yes-men? Staff who'll only tell you what you want to hear, rather than the truth?'

Declan tensed, thrusting his head forward aggressively. 'I assume you have a point? Perhaps you'd like to advise on the Middle Eastern project brief too, since you're such an expert? Or the staffing shortfall in Western Australia? Or the negotiations with government on—'

'There's no need to be sarcastic. You know I have no idea what you're talking about.'

Yet she stood her ground. That was more than

his managers had done in Sydney last week. The realisation intrigued him. She intrigued him.

Declan folded his arms. 'Go on. I'm waiting.'

He heard her shuffle her feet. He'd been right: she was nervous.

'I think you'd be more…productive with one of your secretaries to help while David's away. You won't get through as much work with me helping. I don't know the ropes.'

'I'll teach you.'

'I've got other work to do.'

He tilted his head, trying to pinpoint exactly the expression in her voice. Reluctance, but something else too.

'What's really on your mind, Chloe? Why don't you want to work with me? I look ugly but I promise I don't bite.'

The words rang into silence and to his chagrin what filled Declan's mind was the realisation of how much he'd enjoy nuzzling the soft flesh of Chloe's throat and nipping it with his teeth. Ever since that day in his bathroom he'd been hard put not to think of her sexually.

'You only want me because you're used to me. I'm not a threat. If someone came up here from the Sydney office you'd feel vulnerable about them seeing you as you are.'

Oh, he wanted her all right. But not just because he was used to her. Though why he wanted her, when she continually stood up to him, never giving an inch, he didn't know. Perhaps he'd discovered a weakness for women who challenged him.

'You're becoming a recluse. That's dangerous, Declan.'

He opened his mouth to fire off an angry retort, then registered the wobble of distress as she said his name—as if she was worried. He frowned. He couldn't remember the last time anyone had been concerned for him except in a professional capacity. Doctors, nurses, investors…

That single, unexpected fact saved her from a blast of wrath.

'You're imagining things. I'm not a recluse.' Even as he said it Declan couldn't quite believe he was having this conversation. Perhaps the accident had knocked him off balance more than he'd suspected.

Needing to reassert his authority, he stalked behind his desk and sank into his ergonomic chair, pleased he hadn't needed to feel his way but knew exactly how many paces to every piece of furniture in the room. He swung round to face her. The familiar position gave the illusion of control in an unfamiliar world that threatened every shred of self-possession.

'You're hiding from the world.'

'Hiding? I suppose I was hiding last week when I had all those meetings in Sydney?' And since when did she have the right to express such views?

It took her a while to reply. But she didn't back down. 'That was just an extension of work. You bury yourself in work.'

'In case you hadn't noticed...' his lip curled '...it's devotion to work that's built my business empire.'

'But you use it to hide. You don't see anyone or go out anywhere unless it's business. It's not healthy.' She drew a sharp breath. 'It wouldn't be surprising if the accident had...affected you. Maybe a counsellor—'

Declan shot to his feet. 'Enough! I do *not* need a counsellor. Nor do I need your uninformed advice.'

'I realise you're upset...'

'Insulted is more like,' he murmured under his breath as he braced himself against the desk. The way he'd jumped from his chair had sent a jolt of pain screeching through his bad leg. His fingers curled into tight fists on the desktop. His physical limitations drove him mad.

'It's not insulting to suggest you might need someone to talk to.'

'Because I don't want to be mobbed?' He shook his head, sick of do-gooders telling him what he needed. 'If you'd gone through what I have you might prefer your own company too.'

'But you don't, do you? You're not happy.'

'Give me strength! Are you a psychiatrist now?'

She must have moved even closer. Her voice came from just in front of him. 'I only know that you've been through a lot and hiding yourself away won't help. It could lead to depression.' Her breath hitched.

About to lambast her, Declan stilled, his attention snagging on the word 'depression'. Instantly Adrian came to mind. He must have been depressed to have commited suicide. The thought sliced close to the bone, leaving Declan winded.

His bright, clever kid brother, so depressed he'd chosen to kill himself rather than go on. Declan blinked and drew in a ragged breath. How had he let that happen?

'You know about depression?' His voice was hoarse.

'I knew someone who was…troubled. If he'd had help, it could have made all the difference.'

Like Ade. If only Declan had come here sooner.

He'd been eager to see his brother after so long apart. It had been five months since his last visit to London and over a year since Ade's last visit here. But with the easy assurance of past experience Declan had assumed their relationship hadn't changed. That, despite the physical absence, they were as close as ever.

How wrong he'd been.

Staying on in Asia to wrap up the latest, biggest contract had been a mistake. Letting Adrian persuade him everything was OK had been a mistake.

'Your friend, did he…?'

'I'd rather not discuss it.' Her clipped tone told Declan everything he needed to know. The last of his outrage disintegrated as he realised she'd been motivated by genuine concern and past loss.

Declan sank back into his seat, suppressing a groan of relief as the searing ache in his leg eased.

'I'll tell you what, Chloe, help me in the office six days a week and I'll increase your pay *plus* I'll even let you take me on an outing to the park with a rug over my knees so I don't get a chill.'

'You really are a sarcastic…'

Declan smiled to hear the spark of impatience

in her tone. He discovered he didn't like it when she was sad.

'Deal, Chloe?'

'How could I turn down such an alluring offer?'

CHAPTER FIVE

'WHAT are you chuckling over?'

Chloe looked up to find Declan on the threshold of the kitchen. It was late afternoon, the hour she had off between working with Declan in the study and getting the dinner prepared. Slanting sunlight burnished his dark hair and highlighted his strong face. A smile hovered at the corner of his lips and her heart clutched.

Working with him had led to more than a truce between them. It had produced a camaraderie she'd never have believed possible, given Declan's determination always to be right. Yet behind the driven man, the man who still scared her with his occasional bleakness, she'd discovered a lurking sense of the absurd and a dry wit that kept her on her toes, plus a generosity of spirit. For all his lofty authority he was egalitarian and easy to work with, setting high standards but helping her achieve them. No wonder David adored his job and fretted over being absent so long.

'What is it, Chloe? Some racy gossip magazine?'

'Hardly. It's *Pride and Prejudice.*'

'And that's funny?' He sounded so sceptical she had to share.

'You haven't read it? How's this for an opening: "it is a truth universally acknowledged, that a single man in possession of a good fortune, must be in want of a wife"?'

He gave a humph and crossed his arms over his chest, the epitome of eye-catching masculinity. 'You find that amusing? She's just telling it like it is. Or like the female half of the population pretends it is.'

Chloe tilted her head as she surveyed his expression. It struck her that she took advantage of his blindness time and again to watch him, fascinated not only by the earthy sexuality of his features but by the subtle changes of expression that merely hinted at his thoughts.

'You're so cynical.' She put the well-thumbed paperback down on the window seat.

He shrugged and propped one shoulder against the door jamb as if settling in for a chat.

Chloe knew an illicit thrill of pleasure at the way their relationship had developed. Instead of snapping her head off when she occasionally voiced concern for him, Declan took it in his stride, accepting her in a way he never had before they'd begun working together. She reminded herself it was the ease of a good working relationship, no more. Yet she couldn't help feeling there was something personal in the way he was so easy with her.

'If you were a single man with a fortune you'd understand.'

'You've had women set their caps at you?'

'If that's a quaint way of asking if they've tried to trick me into marriage, then yes. But never with caps. Transparent lingerie is more the norm,' he mused, rubbing his chin. 'Or lace. Or even—'

'I get the picture!' Chloe sat up, discomfited by the idea of so many women—doubtless sophisticated, accomplished women—throwing themselves at him.

A dart of pure jealousy shafted through her, stealing her breath. It was ridiculous when he was her boss, but she still hadn't been able to scotch her attraction to him.

'Attraction'! Such a mealy mouthed word for the searing swirl of awareness that was an ever-present undercurrent. Knowing him better, watching him fight every day, every hour, to find ways around his blindness—pushing himself to the limit with exercises to heal his leg, tackling life as best he could—Chloe felt so much more than desire. There was respect. Admiration. Sympathy. And more.

She felt…too much. Even without putting a name to it, surely what she felt for Declan was too much, too soon?

How had he sneaked past her defences? She'd been content for so long, living her quiet, contained life. He challenged her, invaded her space, made her think and *feel*.

She remembered the toll Mark's loss had taken and knew real fear.

By comparison this was no gently nurtured sentiment but a fierce alloy of emotions forged so deep in her soul she shied from dwelling on it.

'At least my condition means I've been spared that for a while.' He sighed. 'Sooner or later some enterprising female will decide I'm an ideal target for matrimony. Poor Declan with his scars and his blindness—he'd be grateful for a little female attention. Easy to dupe too.'

'Don't talk like that.' Chloe surged to her feet, her hands fisting at her sides.

'Sorry.' His tone was short. 'I don't usually wallow in self-pity.'

'It's not that.' Her voice was uneven as she strove to breathe normally. 'It's…' She shook her head, unable to put into words the protective emotion filling her. She hated it when he spoke of himself as less than he was, as an object of pity.

'You're too canny to be conned. You're a good judge of character.'

'You think? Not always. I've made mistakes.' He scowled and she guessed he was thinking of his brother. She'd seen and heard enough to know he blamed himself for not being here when Adrian had needed him. That knowledge made him all the more human. More likeable.

'You'll fall in love one day and that will be it.'

'Love?' His brows rose. 'I doubt it.'

'You don't believe in love?' The idea shocked her. Love had been what turned her life around. Her foster parents' love, then Mark's. Without that she'd still be the angry, anti-social victim she'd believed herself as a teenager, hiding a sense of inadequacy behind bravado. Love was the one solid comfort when the world turned bleak.

'And you do?'

'I do.'

Was it his imagination that her words sounded like a vow?

Declan tried to summon the sceptical attitude that had seen him through years of success in the cut-throat world of international construction, countless grasping females and a false paternity suit. He sought the words to deny her certainty but, to his amazement, couldn't find them.

Instead he wondered what it would be like to have a woman like Chloe—forthright, honest and sexy as hell—believe she was in love with him.

Heat sizzled along his veins. His belly hollowed with something like excitement. Almost as if he *wanted* the picture she painted: the love of one woman.

A woman like Chloe?

He rubbed the back of his neck. What the hell was happening to him? He'd even taken to following her, needing her presence more and more to fill the void of emptiness.

He marched across the kitchen, flicked the switch on the kettle and reached for the tea caddy on the bench just below the window.

'How did you do that?'

Chloe's voice arrested him as he was in the middle of levering the top off the caddy.

'Do what?' If she was going to cross-question him about his views on love and marriage…

'Find the tea caddy so easily.'

Her words trickled into his consciousness and his heart gave an almighty thump.

How had he known it was there? The kettle needed no explanation. Chloe was meticulous in putting it back in exactly the same position so he could find it easily when he wanted it. But usually it was coffee he wanted, not tea.

There was a metallic clunk as the container slipped from his hands to the bench. His fingers spasmed as if trying too late to retrieve it.

Declan blinked but the unrelieved blankness gave no clue. Except that he could have sworn he remembered seeing light and darkness, sunlight and shadow, a moment before. As if the edge of the window where the caddy rested had been high-lighted.

Impossible.

Yet his breath hissed in as he relived the illusion.

'Could you...*see* something?' Chloe's voice, soft and hopeful, came from right behind him. He felt her presence and inhaled her vanilla scent.

But before him was nothing but blackness.

Fury scorched him, incinerating the tiny bud of hope that had, for a moment, begun to unfurl. His fist thumped the counter. Bad enough to be blind, but to have the doctors keep hope alive, saying there was no reason he shouldn't regain his sight—it was too much!

Better to kill hope dead than face continual disappointment. He couldn't live like that. Nor could he hold out false hope to this woman who had come to mean so much.

'Of course not,' he snarled. 'I can't see a damned thing. You know that.'

Her silence was heavy with words left unsaid and Declan knew regret for lashing out.

It wasn't Chloe's fault. A better man would apologise, would explain. But, he realised as emotion grabbed his throat and stifled his larynx, he was scared what he might blurt out to her if once he started.

With Chloe he felt…different. He wanted more, though he managed to hide it most of the time.

'I have something for you.' Her voice was calm, blessed relief from his turbulent emotions.

'You do?' As ever, he turned towards her voice.

'Here.' She pressed something into his palm and closed his fingers around it.

Declan swallowed hard, unmoving. In all these weeks he hadn't touched her. Not since that day in his bathroom when the mere feel of her hand in his, the caress of her soft cheek, had almost blown his mind and his good intentions.

Now, without knowing it, she'd just unleashed the howling need he'd rammed into a dark corner of his soul, carefully guarded with every protection wit and hard work could provide.

A great shudder racked him and his hand shook in hers.

'Declan? Are you all right?'

'Fine,' he croaked. 'What is it?'

'You'll like it,' she assured him brightly. A shade too brightly. 'It's a sensor. You slip it over the rim of your mug. Here.' She guided his hand to a mug he heard her take from the cupboard. 'Put it on the lip, then when the water boils you make sure you've got the spout above the cup and pour. The sensor beeps when the water reaches it so you won't overflow the mug. Cool, eh?'

Declan felt her shift away. The warmth of her skin faded from his and he knew loss so profound it terrified him. He wanted to haul her back and hold her close. He wanted to keep her with him, the one bright spot in his murky world. She made life bearable.

'Declan?'

'Thanks, Chloe.' He forced his lips into a tight smile. 'It's perfect. No blind man should be without one.'

Chloe floated on her back in the heated pool. The sun had set in glory over the mountains and only the pool lights illuminated the scene. She should be in bed after another taxing day but she couldn't sleep.

Because of Declan.

He was always on her mind: his restless energy, his piercing intellect, his surprising humour once he lowered his guard enough to let her know the real man, his insight and understanding. Working with him daily, she was no longer surprised to discover he funded his staff to build clinics in India, a hospital in Haiti and wells in Africa, as well as taking on prestigious commercial projects. He didn't suffer fools but he was generous and had a conscience some of her previous employers had lacked.

Employers. She sucked in a quick breath. That taboo had crumbled before the force of her feelings.

She saw him as a man, not a boss.

Declan Carstairs had a dark intensity that made her shiver even as it tugged her closer.

He wasn't like Mark—gentle and decent in a quiet, unassuming way.

Declan was larger than life, demanding all her attention, stretching her, challenging her. Making her feel different. She liked and respected him and his pain, so carefully hidden, haunted her.

His unspoken grief forced her to confront her negative memories of his brother and wonder about the man Adrian had been at heart, before illness had changed him.

Declan's grief for his brother did him credit, proof of his deep capacity for love.

Love?

Her mind froze. She couldn't, *mustn't* think in those terms. Heart pounding, she tried to focus instead on the moment.

Chloe spread her fingers, letting water slide past. It was like swimming in liquid silk, the water caressing her hyper-sensitive body. A body Declan Carstairs had brought to life after six years of hibernation.

It frightened her that she couldn't thrust him from her mind.

She couldn't silence the voice of desire that whispered Declan's name in a litany of need. He'd smashed through the careful equilibrium she'd painstakingly built since losing Mark.

Too often she found herself longing to hold him, cradle him in her arms and ease his pain. Or let the flames of desire consume them.

It was as well David Sarkesian was due back soon. She'd miss the intimate sessions listening to Declan's voice, feeling it ripple across her senses like a call to heady pleasure. They worked in tandem, attuned to each other as if they'd done it for years.

Her feelings were too dangerous.

Soon she'd be safe. Not from Declan, but from her own longings.

The flagstones were warm from the long-vanished sun when Declan limped out of the house, stride lengthening as he approached the pool.

An instant later, arms overhead in a long, smooth dive he was airborne. That moment of heady anticipation was the closest he got to a thrill now extreme sports were denied him.

Water closed around him and, for a millisecond, he knew familiar regret at its safe embrace. How much simpler to throw himself over the edge and find not water but an end.

But Declan wasn't his brother. No matter how heavy the burden, he couldn't wish himself dead. Even now, half the man he was, weighed by guilt, there was too much to do. If not for himself, then to find justice for Adrian.

That was why sleep eluded him.

It had nothing to do with another day working with Chloe, her scent tickling his nose, her voice an invitation to pleasure.

What had David been thinking, hiring a woman whose voice, when she forgot to sound like Miss Prim, was sultry and beckoning?

For too long Declan had clamped down on unruly needs and wayward thoughts, on the seductive image of Chloe beside him, not just in the office but in his life. It was crazy but he'd found himself contemplating a relationship—not a brief sexual liaison, but a long-term partnership.

The sort of old-fashioned relationship he'd never had time for.

What kind of fool was he? Had blindness clouded his mind?

No woman in her right mind, much less a woman as bright, alluring and intelligent as Chloe, would tie herself to a scarred shadow of a man. Only a woman motivated by pity or greed could overlook what he'd become: a cripple, unable to do the smallest tasks without aid. A man who was hollow at the core, unworthy of love, unable to protect those most precious.

He didn't need pity.

He needed to work himself into exhaustion.

Declan's head broke the surface; he hauled his arm out of the water and brought it down in a stroke that collided with something floating in the pool.

Not something. Someone.

Automatically he righted himself. Slick flesh was beneath his hands; ripe contours of hip and waist; the heat of a breast against his chest. Long legs tangling with his.

His hold firmed at her waist, slipping into the neat indentation with a proprietorial ease that should have disturbed him. Instead it sent a jolt of instant pleasure to his groin. He kicked, keeping them both afloat, and again felt the slide of smooth legs between his.

Heat spiralled low like a rope pulling tight.

'Chloe?'

What other mermaid would invade his private domain?

She moved as he raised his hand, and he brushed one sweetly curved breast. The pebble-hardness of her nipple teased his palm.

Instinctively he cupped her breast, loving the fit of her in his hold, hearing her gasp through a veil of pounding sound as his pulse revved into gear. Did she push against his touch?

'Declan!' It was a soft plea. To his straining ears it sounded like a plea for more. Brutally he reminded himself it couldn't be. It had to be surprise, disgust.

Sanity seeped in and he dragged his hand away

to grasp her arm instead. His palm felt branded by her breast, the outline of its perfect nub still teasing him.

Again her legs brushed his, only this time his erection got in the way. Heat slicked his skin.

Her indrawn breath was loud. She stopped moving. Was she frozen in horror?

Declan reminded himself he had every right to swim naked. It was late at night. This was *his* pool, his place of solitude and solace. *She* was the interloper. He'd come here to avoid thinking of her.

His lips twisted. Everywhere he turned she was there. His senses had taken on a preternatural keenness, even able to discern her humming from the other side of the house. She drove him insane. He didn't know which was worse: unrequited lust or the impossible dreams of long-term togetherness that corroded his commonsense.

'Are you OK?' he growled.

'Of course I'm OK.' Yet her voice was muffled, as if she had trouble getting her breath.

His own breathing had shallowed and his chest pounded.

'What are you doing here?' His voice, caught low in his throat, was gruff.

'Swimming. Well, floating. Relaxing.' Her voice was stilted, edgy. Who could blame her?

He tried to imagine her floating. Light hair and pale skin, she'd said. He imagined platinum hair rayed out, skin like moonlight, limbs spread as if waiting for him to come to her.

Inevitably frustration bubbled up. He wanted to see her for himself! He wanted...

'Declan.' Her voice whispered across raw nerves. 'You need to let me go.'

He tried yet his fingers held fast.

'You're not struggling to get away.' Amazingly she was pliant in his grip.

Because she feared what he might do? Did she recognise the beast within?

'Do I need to?' Her voice had a husky edge that sent shivers of pleasure to his groin.

'It would help.' His own voice thickened. 'But don't worry. I won't hurt you.'

'I never thought you would.'

A brittle laugh escaped him. Such trust.

He needed a workout to exhaust him just so he could put her from his mind. He was too aware of her sweet, yielding flesh. He was so hungry, so needy. Not for just any woman; that was the curse and the piquancy of it. For *this* woman. The one who'd driven him to the edge of sanity. Who'd incited impossible yearnings.

He'd never felt so out of control nor so unsure of himself.

'Declan?' A hand touched his face, cupped his jaw, her thumb resting on the hated scar. 'Are you all right?'

He didn't intend to tilt his face against her palm, but somehow he was leaning in.

'Perfect,' he lied. He teetered on a knife edge. 'Why aren't you getting out?'

Her hand slid from his face. He was so desperate, he almost believed the move was reluctant.

'You're still holding me.'

Of course; he had to release her. Grimly he dragged his hand from her arm till he held her only at the waist. He needed to unhook his arm but couldn't quite manage it.

He kicked slowly, keeping them afloat, and again his naked length brushed her. A shudder snaked down his spine and shot to his groin.

'Declan!'

'Sorry. It was unintentional.'

Was it? He yearned to press against her soft body, into her secret warmth. He longed to taste her.

'It's getting late,' she whispered. 'I should…'

It was a platitude he recognised. He sought relief in anger, knowing it was safer than anything else he felt.

'Run away?' he snarled. 'I don't blame you. Looking at my ugly face must be a trial. I...'

Her hand at his collarbone sucked the words away.

'Chloe?' She palmed his chest. It wasn't the touch of a woman who wanted to escape. Tentative, yes, but with a thoroughness that awakened every nerve ending.

'You're not ugly.' Again that throaty edge to her voice. 'I've wanted to touch you...'

'You have?' Astonishment made him reel, but not for long. Before she could come to her senses he kissed her neck and revelled in the pulse he found there pattering out of control. She tasted of salt water and sweet, vanilla-spiced Chloe.

'You should go inside.'

'I should want to leave.' Her voice trembled.

'Chloe?' Was he hearing things? Imagining what he wanted to hear?

But it was beyond him to push her away. With a groan, he captured her mouth.

He couldn't remember experiencing such a kiss before. Blindness made each sense more acute. She was sheer delight. He felt her smooth heat, each tiny tremble, smelled the fresh scent of her damp skin and devoured her sweetness—unique and addictive.

She pressed close, giving back kiss for kiss in a cycle that grew from tentative to lush, from slow to hungry.

Only the feel of water closing over their heads drew him back to sanity. Almost to sanity.

Urgently Declan propelled them through the water till they reached the shallow end of the pool. The water fell to thigh height and still he held her against him.

Each second he expected rejection, knew it was inevitable. Instead, he felt tiny ripples of arousal course through her. His pulse galloped. She kept one arm roped across his shoulders as the other slid down his abdomen.

'Don't.' His voice was a strangled burr. 'Not unless you want this over before it begins.'

Her hand slipped away and fear scudded through him.

'Do you want this, Chloe? Do you want me?' Once he'd never have asked such a question. Once he'd been confident, even blasé about sex. But now, disabled and scarred, doubt racked him.

He was so lost without his vision. He couldn't even read her face. Tension gnawed at his belly; uncertainty.

'I want you, Declan.' It was the voice of a siren, low and intoxicating. 'I want…'

The rest of her words ended in a gasp as he lowered her onto a wide step and placed his hand, broad and sure, over that sweet spot between her legs. He felt her response as he took her mouth hungrily.

Fire was in his blood, anticipation in every taut muscle. He'd only just sunk into her embrace, his fingers slipping beneath her bikini to find the nub of her pleasure, when she jolted in his arms, limbs stiffening.

He swallowed her gasp of astonishment, felt the heavy pulse of delight at her centre, and then she was arching up against his hand, coming apart against his touch with an innocent ferocity that staggered him.

'Declan!' Her voice was a stunned thread of sound that circled his senses, ensnaring and bewitching. She clutched him as if he was the one solid point in her world and his chest swelled with emotion.

He tasted her lips and her desperate enthusiasm drew him close to the edge. She was so hungry, so ready. That was an intoxication greater than any he'd known.

'It's been a long time for you,' he murmured.

He'd never known a woman so desperate for him. For sex, he amended. Yet the idea that she responded to him alone had a subversive glamour he couldn't quite dismiss.

'Too long.' She pressed her lips to his, swirled her tongue between his lips. 'Years.'

Years? After just a few months of celibacy Declan was climbing the walls with frustration.

That explained why she was willing to ignore his scarred features. Right now he almost didn't care—he was so grateful for her eagerness and warm, responsive body.

Resting his weight on one elbow, he dragged the bikini bottom away. She reached for him but he brushed her hand aside. Time for that later.

It was the work of a moment to lift her higher on the steps so only her shins were submerged. Then he settled himself, low enough that her inner thighs were wet silk against his stubble. For a moment he wondered if his skin might be too rough, until she moaned and clutched his hair, drawing him to her.

'Chloe, you're driving me insane.' The words were muffled against her skin as his body responded with a surge of heady arousal. She tasted delicious, sweet and salt. Her legs, cool and smooth, closed round him and she raised herself, a gift to be savoured.

One kiss and she sighed. One slow flick of the tongue and her fingers tightened like talons in his hair. Declan didn't mind. He didn't want to be anywhere but here.

He nuzzled her tender skin and she moaned his name in that throaty plea he could become addicted to.

'You like that?'

'You know I do. I can't…'

Her words trailed off as he caressed her again, felt the tiny tremor of pleasure wash through her like a wave.

Declan smiled, savouring the taste of arousal, enjoying her reactions and the open, intensely exciting way she embraced pleasure.

Had sex ever been so simple, so satisfying? His body throbbed hard in anticipation.

One more slow, provocative kiss and the tremor became a quake that rocked her body, dragged the breath from her lungs in a shout of ecstasy. He tasted her pleasure, her thrumming pulse, and revelled in the feel of her finally relaxing in delight around him.

He lifted himself higher, pressed a kiss to one delicious breast. Another to her parted lips as she lay gasping for air. She was still, supine and spent.

On a tide of energy Declan got to his feet. He

reached down to pull her up then stopped as sanity hit him with the cool night air.

Doubt stirred. Harsh reality. He sucked in a gasping breath as his brain engaged.

She'd been desperate for release. The merest touch had unravelled her. Would she still want him now, with the edge taken off her hunger? Or would his scars deter her? It was one thing to take what was offered, another to desire actively. He wanted her to come to him willingly, eyes open and sure, not out of pity or gratitude or indebtedness.

He couldn't bear the thought of her averting her eyes while he made love to her.

Declan stepped from the pool before he could have second thoughts. Water sluiced around him and for one unsteady moment he could have sworn he saw the fuzzy outline of the pool's rim lit by submerged lights.

Then the unrelenting blackness closed around him, a reminder that hope was fake.

Even so he refused to beg for scraps. Pride rose, his one defence.

'I'm going to my room.' His voice was thick. 'You know where to find me if you want me.'

CHAPTER SIX

SHE wasn't coming.

Ridiculous to be so disappointed.

He'd convinced himself Chloe wanted him as he did her. More, that they shared something even stronger—an understanding, a connection he couldn't put a name to.

He'd been a wishful fool.

Stupid not to have taken what was offered when he'd had the chance. He'd let pride interfere, convincing him Chloe must come to him so he could be sure she wanted *him*, not just an anonymous orgasm in the dark.

Now he cursed his ego. If he'd stayed, at least he'd have had release, pride or no pride.

His body ached with arousal. It would ache for days to come.

For weeks he'd considered finding a woman to ease the burn of need but hadn't followed through. It was Chloe he wanted. Chloe he needed. Not some sympathetic ex-girlfriend or stranger.

His jaw throbbed with tension and he cursed under his breath. This couldn't go on. One of them would have to go. Tomorrow he'd...

The sound of the door opening stopped all thought.

'Chloe?' Was that his voice—that husk of sound?

'It's me, Declan.'

His chest expanded mightily as he drew his first unfettered breath since leaving the pool. The weight between his shoulders lifted and the swirl of agitation in his belly morphed into a pulse of anticipation.

'You came.'

'How could I not?' Her voice curled around him, filling him with an unfamiliar sensation. Relief? Joy?

He shook his head, telling himself his imagination ran riot, blaming it on sexual frustration.

'Because you feel you owe me.' He gritted his teeth, so close to losing control he feared he wouldn't be able to hold back, even if she admitted she was here out of pity.

'No.' She paused and he could swear he heard her breath on the night air. 'Because I want you.'

Her words scooped the breath from his lungs, leaving him hollow and strangely vulnerable.

Was he really so desperate? It terrified him how

much he needed that to be true. How much he needed from her.

'Doing it with a blind man turns you on, does it?' The words ripped out of his mouth before he could stop them.

Chloe stifled a gasp as his words grazed like shattered glass across tender skin.

Didn't he want her here?

Even now, seeing his rampant arousal as he stood naked in the light, she was tempted to turn tail. Hide again inside her shell of routine and profess-ionalism and measured responses designed to keep emotions at a distance.

Yet she stood rooted to the spot.

She needed Declan like she needed to draw her next breath.

Lust, yes, but far more too.

It was too late to go back. It had been too late from the moment Declan had taken her in his arms.

She understood now that much of his anger was self-directed. Frustration at his limitations kept him on edge and ready to lash out.

Chloe told herself the rigidity in his big frame was from tension, not distaste. She'd felt his hands tremble with need before he'd abandoned her.

Yet it took all her strength to face him, letting her presence brazenly declare her need. She'd been gutted when he left, overwhelmed by doubts and fears as well as cravings she barely understood.

Declan Carstairs made her feel too much.

Her hands shook and the tray rattled.

'What's that?'

'A tray. Wine. Food.' As she spoke she walked to the other side of the king-sized bed and placed it on the hand-carved dresser. Holding the tray reminded her of her place in his household. Her paid role.

But tonight she wasn't his housekeeper. She firmed her lips, reminding herself they'd come together as equals.

'You're trying to turn this into some romantic encounter?' His mouth lifted in a sneering smile that cut her to the core. She stilled, heart thumping.

'You didn't eat dinner and I thought you might be hungry.' For the life of her Chloe wouldn't admit that preparing the trappings of a romantic tryst had calmed her rioting nerves.

Even after her abandoned behaviour in the pool, she had difficulty facing her desperate need for this man. She didn't do quick, meaningless sex.

Was she fooling herself believing there was more to this than sex?

'Are you this abrasive with everyone?' She planted her hands on her hips and stared at him across the bed. 'So eager for confrontation?' He looked magnificent, tall, powerfully muscled, outrageously virile. But he was an emotional minefield.

'Or is it that you don't want *me*, Declan, because I'm a mere employee?' Finally her own anger exploded. 'Is that it? You don't think I'm good enough for you?'

This man had shattered the barriers that had protected her feelings for six years. He'd broken through the impenetrable distance that had kept her safe and content. She hadn't wanted to care about him, much less want him. She resented the way he'd turned her into a woman she barely recognised.

'Of course I want you! What do you think this is?' He lowered one hand to cup his impressive erection and her mouth dried as a jolt of sexual arousal quaked through her.

She wanted to hold him there, feel the velvet-soft flesh over iron-hard erection. Her damp palms clenched and the pulse humming between her legs notched up to a heavy, needy beat.

'Then what's your problem?' Her voice was choked. 'Are you scared I'll expect more than you're willing to give? Do you think when the sun comes up tomorrow I'll forget my lowly place in your employ?'

Adrian Carstairs had tried to use her paid position as a lever to get her into his bed, at first cajoling and then threatening.

'I don't give a damn about your position.' Declan's voice was a lethal growl as he paced closer to the bed.

'Then why don't you like me?' Her chin tilted defiantly.

'Like?' It was a raw shout. 'Who says I don't like you?'

His hands fisted at his sides and, despite her anger and confusion, Chloe felt something inside melt at the erotically masculine picture he made. There was an elemental rawness, an unvarnished power that emanated from Declan even when dressed in a tailored suit. Now—naked, angry and aroused—he was breathtaking.

Dampness bloomed at the apex of Chloe's thighs and her pulse accelerated.

'If it's not me, then it must be you,' she shot back. 'What are you scared of, Declan?'

'I don't do scared.' Yet she saw emotion ripple across his features, catching at his scar and stiffening that side of his face.

Instantly her anger doused. There was something there…something troubling him…but he'd never admit it.

'Then prove it. Get on the bed.'

For an instant shock froze his features, then his lips curved up in a smile that looked more pain that pleasure. 'What? You want to minister to the cripple's needs? How magnanimous of you.'

Something thwacked her hard in the solar plexus. Her chest tightened in a vicious cramp as she realised he truly saw himself as an object of pity. Tenderness welled with regret at how his accident had skewed his self-belief.

He was more virile, more attractive, more real and strong than any man she'd ever known.

Did he truly think she'd come here out of pity? She shook her head, her hair swirling around her shoulders.

Declan Carstairs had turned her world on its head with the sheer force of his personality, making her feel emotions she'd never wanted or hoped to experience again. She was fast falling in love and he thought she felt sorry for him!

'You're no more a cripple than I am. But if it makes you feel better let's pretend this has nothing to do with you.' Pain speared her. 'Let's just say I'm here to satisfy my own needs.' She hauled in a difficult breath, guessing if she revealed her feelings he'd turn away in an instant. 'Does that make it easier for you and your ego?'

'Chloe, I—'

'Don't, Declan. Please.' Suddenly she felt stretched too thin, her control fragile. Chloe wrapped her arms around herself, as if to hold in the tensions tearing her apart.

She couldn't take much more. She faced needs and emotions that stunned her, that had erupted out of nowhere in her safe, stable world. Plus she confronted Declan's hidden demons that she could only guess at.

'I'm sorry.'

Her gaze jerked back to his face, now solemn and calm.

'I *do* want you, Chloe. I've been going crazy these last weeks, trying to hold back.' His voice was hypnotically deep and enthralling, tugging her closer. His big hands clenched and unclenched at his sides as if seeking outlet for the raw tension within him.

'The question is, do you really want *me*?'

She shook her head that he even had to ask. 'I do.' The words sounded solemn in the silent room. 'Absolutely.'

His unseeing eyes focused on her as if seeking confirmation. Then he stepped forward, walking to the side of the bed. With one quick movement he climbed up and settled himself on his back, palms flat on the bedspread.

Heat fluttered in her stomach. From his torn leg and scarred cheek, to his thick dark hair and determined chin, he was more desirable than any man had a right to be.

Her heart squeezed at the vulnerability he strove to hide. At his proud, almost arrogant attitude that was no façade but part of the essential Declan. He was a man of depth and subtlety, of strength and secrets as well as charisma and sex appeal. He was the man who'd torn apart her defences and laid her heart bare.

It was on the tip of her tongue to ask if he was sure, her own doubts rearing up. But she bit back the words. Slowly she paced around the bed, feeling the swish of gossamer-fine fabric against her aroused body.

'Tell me what you're wearing.' His voice rippled across her skin.

Declan folded his hands behind his head. The movement accentuated the broad muscles of his shoulders and arms. Her breath caught at the sight of all that leashed power waiting for her.

'A robe.'

'Silk.'

'How can you tell?' She hesitated, suddenly uncertain. He stared directly at her, almost as if he saw her.

He shrugged and her mouth dried. She imagined those strong shoulders cradling her. 'It sounds like silk, like a whisper against your skin when you walk.'

She shook her head. She couldn't hear what he did, her senses hampered by the roar of blood in her ears.

'You look beautiful.'

Chloe smiled even as her breath snared. 'You don't know how I look.' She'd never been glamorous despite her unusual colouring. She doubted he'd give her a second glance if he could see.

'I know your face, remember?' His chest expanded mightily on a satisfied smile. 'You let me touch you. I remember your soft skin; your neat, straight nose and the bow of your lips. They're full, aren't they, Chloe—pouting and ready to be kissed?'

Sparks of heat flared in a twisting coil as his words curled around her. Her lips parted, tingling, as if waiting for the caress of his mouth.

'You'd look more beautiful without the wrap,' he murmured. 'Take it off.'

The sheer wanton thrill of his words stifled

thought. He seduced her just with that rich growl that scraped like cut velvet across aroused flesh.

'*Now*, Chloe. I want you naked.'

Her fingers were unsteady as she fumbled with the knot at her waist. Finally it loosened. She shrugged and the robe slithered to the floor.

Declan's smile widened. 'Excellent. Now come to me.'

Chloe was already climbing onto the bed, her heart hammering high in her throat. 'Stop giving orders, Declan. You're not my boss now.'

She knelt over him, hands flat on the black and gold silk cover she'd smoothed across the vast bed only this morning. Bending, she pressed a kiss to his knee, feeling the tickle of coarse hair. Another kiss, a few centimetres higher, and his skin twitched and tightened.

Her third kiss brushed the scar that scored his thigh.

'Don't!' Strong hands reached for her but she resisted their pull. 'You don't have to. Not there.'

'My turn, Declan.' She didn't even care that he'd hear the breathless excitement in her strangled voice. She pressed another kiss, higher this time, to the heavy muscle of his thigh. It jumped beneath her lips and his fingers tunnelled into her hair, grasping and tangling.

'Like silk,' he murmured, and Chloe knew a flash of triumph that the sound was an uneven gasp. This desperate magic was shared. He was as unravelled by it as she.

She nuzzled his inner thigh and he froze. The hiss of his breath was loud in her ears.

Chloe smiled as she centred herself over him. 'Not so bossy now, are you?' Then her hand was on him, smoothing hot satin over iron-hard arousal. Her mouth followed, a gentle kiss at first, before she let her tongue lave the full, impressive length of him.

Fire ignited at her core and the hungry pulse between her legs clenched hard and tight.

She wanted…

'No.' Declan grabbed her shoulders and yanked her up high. 'You can't.'

Chloe revelled in the hard weight of his hands on her flesh, the heat of him beneath her, and the stark tension in his face. All for *her*.

'I can, Declan. I want to.' It was true. One taste and she craved more. She licked her lips, savouring the salt-and-spice taste of him.

But his grip firmed as he shook his head.

'No.' It was a hoarse whisper. 'I can't last if you do that.'

His face was taut, skin stretched across strong

bones. He looked to be in pain. Tenderness welled within her and she cupped his jaw. The rasp of tiny bristles sensitised her skin.

Leaning forward, she whispered, 'Do you need to last?' The notion of Declan Carstairs yielding utterly to the magic of the moment filled her with heady excitement. 'I want you to lose control.'

She slid her hand down and curled her fingers around him.

He pulsed in her hold. Excitement blasted through her at his latent power and the fact that the pair of them together felt so *right*.

'Wait!' The order came through clenched teeth as he rolled on his side and reached for the bed-side table. Reluctantly she released him. When he turned back he was sheathed and her heart gave a quick jump. She could scarcely believe she was giving herself to a man for the first time in six years. The only man since…

But there could be no second thoughts. Sharing herself with Declan was as inevitable as the sun rising in the morning.

She pressed her lips to his jaw, needing his scent in her nostrils, his taste on her tongue.

He tugged her down onto his body. His erection nudged her entrance, hot and thick, and a shiver of heat ripped through her. Chloe eased back as

Declan rose beneath her and in slow motion the moment went on and on. Carefully, almost gently, he filled her aching void till she trembled on the brink of an awareness she'd never before known.

She quivered around him, her hands unsteady as she gripped his hard shoulders for balance.

'Chloe.' The word was a whisper. He sounded as stupefied as she felt. Nothing in her memory could match the word-stealing beauty of the moment.

Internal muscles clenched and abruptly the breathless moment shattered. Declan clamped his hands at her hips, surging high, and she gasped at the exquisite pleasure of his possession.

At his urging she sat back, knees spread around him. His hands went unerringly to her breasts, evoking ecstasy with the brush of hard fingers on crested nipples.

This floodtide of sensation, of desperate need and eager response was overwhelming. Declan urged her higher, faster, and she complied eagerly, fingers curling over his as he held her.

The pressure built with each thrust of his hips, each hungry slide of body on body. Chloe felt branded, possessed, yet cherished. Declan's powerful hands caressed her tenderly even as he pumped into her body with an urgent desperation that matched her own.

'I'm sorry,' he gasped. 'I can't…wait.' His pulsing length filled her and the fire exploded within,
toppling her over the edge into ecstasy.

'Kiss me.' Her voice in the darkness roused him
from the stupor of bliss that left him boneless.
'Please.'

She didn't sound like his crisply efficient housekeeper. She sounded…like he felt: drowsy, sated
and stunned. As if the world had tilted on its axis
and not returned to normal. For a moment he almost believed he saw shadow and light shimmer
in his long-dead vision.

Then her hands cupped his shoulders and long,
soft tresses spilled around his neck and shoulders.
Instantly nerve endings that had all but been obliterated by that cataclysmic orgasm tingled into life.
Declan's hands slid from her hips to her waist,
closing there as if they belonged.

'I love your hair,' he whispered. 'You should
wear it down all the time.' Then he could run his
fingers through it at will, tangle his fist in it and
draw her close whenever he desired.

He desired her continually. Working with her,
not touching her, had been torture.

He heard the smile in her voice as she leaned

near, her breath a tantalising puff of air on his face. 'It would get in the way.'

'I don't care.' Unable to resist, he caught long locks in one hand. 'I like it.'

'And what you want goes, is that it? I—'

'You talk too much,' he growled, tugging her to him. Unerringly her lips, petal-soft and delicious, met his.

A tremor shook him. Her mouth accommodated his, opening eagerly as he thrust his tongue in to delve between her sweet lips. It struck him abruptly that kissing Chloe was unlike anything he'd shared before.

Her taste was addictive. He anchored her head to him with one hand and plunged deep.

Their kiss was lush, slow and thorough. A mating of mouths that sent thoughts spiralling out of control and senses tumbling.

Women enjoyed kissing, so Declan had mastered the art early, learning to seduce and please in the lead up to the physical gratification that was his goal. Yet now this easy skill, a way of pleasing a woman and pandering to her desire for closeness, became something else.

A groan of hunger escaped him. Declan needed this kiss as much as she. He clutched her close, savouring the sheer pleasure of Chloe's lips on his, their breaths mingling. Joy rose, full and heavy in his chest.

In the dark, surrounded by her scent and taste, Declan experienced a closeness he'd never before known. As if his secret yearnings were made real.

Determination solidified in him. She *would* be his. Not just for one night.

CHAPTER SEVEN

CHLOE woke to grey skies and the sound of drumming rain. It was late, far too late to lie in bed.

Vaguely she remembered surfacing early, replete and warm in Declan's arms, only to find passion awakening as he feathered kisses over her face and throat.

Her pulse throbbed at the memory of their dawn love-making. Declan had been intent, his movements slow and devastatingly thorough, till she'd screamed her release, clutching him close. She'd fallen into blissful sleep moments after his climax made him slump, spent, in her arms.

She'd never slept as soundly as she had in Declan's bed.

But it must be mid-morning. She slid cautiously towards the side of the bed, trying not to wake him.

A hand on her upper arm stopped her.

'Where are you going?' Even drowsy, his voice held a deep, commanding timbre that tickled every sense.

'It's time I got up. It's late.'

'Don't go.' He hauled her back, wrapped his arm around her and turned her towards him.

She loved being cocooned against him, safe in his strong embrace. Her body relaxed like a cat cuddling into warmth. At the brush of wiry chest hair against sensitised breasts a jolt of response arrowed to her pelvis.

Chloe shook her head. How many times had they made love? Still her body melted whenever they touched. Surely that compulsion should have eased? This was all too new and unfamiliar. She needed time to find her balance.

Even as she thought it, he moved and the hot slide of his erection stroked her thigh.

'You're incorrigible!'

'Is that a complaint?' She loved the lazy chuckle in his voice, even though it turned her insides to mush. It was wonderful to hear him smile.

'No, but I need to get up. I can't stay here all day.' Though the idea was tempting.

'Why? What's so important?'

'The usual chores—cleaning, cooking, a trip to the shops. All the things a housekeeper does.'

'Nothing that can't wait.' He stroked a finger down her cheek and she almost purred aloud. She was so attuned to him, physically as well as emotionally. 'Except the shops. We'll go later; I've almost run out of condoms.'

Chloe choked on a gasp of laughter. The pulse between her legs quickened, shocking her anew.

For years she'd forgotten physical passion existed. Now she was at its mercy because of Declan.

She looked into his wickedly amused face, noting again how he seemed to meet her gaze though he couldn't see her. It was as if, even blind, he sensed so much about her.

Did he sense that, despite the stunning sex, for her this wasn't just about the physical? That what she felt for him grew perilously close to true caring?

'I really should get up.' She tried for crisp and decisive, but her voice came out wobbly.

'Why? Is your ogre of a boss going to give you the third degree over why you're late?'

One side of his mouth tilted up in a smile that tugged her chest tight. It was so rare, so precious, she wanted to savour it.

'My ogre of a boss probably has a stack of new emails for me to check. After I've cooked our breakfast.'

'Mmm, breakfast. Now you mention it, I *am* hungry.' He lowered his head to her breast, sucking at the nipple till it stood erect, then nipping it with a gentle bite that sent every nerve ending into shivering overdrive.

'Declan.' Half-heartedly she pushed at his shoulders, distracted by the sensations he evoked. Finally he pulled back, heat simmering in the depths of his dark eyes.

'Maybe you're right about breakfast. What food is there on that tray you brought last night?'

'Fruit. You'll need something more substantial. I'll go and—'

'You're not going anywhere, Chloe. Not yet.' He tightened his hold. 'Are you always this dedicated to your job or are you looking for a reason to escape?' The humour left his voice and his brows drew down in a familiar frown. She wanted to reach up and smooth it away. It reminded her of his raw reaction last night when he'd thought himself the object of pity. What they shared was so fragile.

'Of course I don't want to escape.' Couldn't he tell by the way her body curled into his, her fingers threading through his thick, dark locks?

Slowly she released her hold and let her hand slide away. What she felt was so intense, so confusing. These weeks had been an emotional roller coaster that had thrown them closer with each sweeping turn. If she was sensible she'd find time away from him to sort out her feelings.

But she didn't want to be sensible. Didn't want to consider the barriers between them—his status and power or her role as his employee.

'It's just that I've got a job to do.'

'Take the day off. Boss's orders.' He stroked a finger across her lips to silence her protest. He lay back and pulled her close, settling her head on his shoulder and wrapping his other hand possessively around her waist.

He wanted her company as much as her body, she realised, remembering how he sought her out even when he didn't have work for her. Trembling excitement flared. Perhaps some of what she felt was shared.

'How did you come to be a housekeeper, anyway? Aren't you a bit young?'

'Old housekeepers must have been young once.'

He shrugged and the movement drew her closer. Chloe breathed deep, addicted to the spicy scent of his skin.

'Most of them come to the job after keeping house for their husbands and families.'

She'd shared a flat with Mark, but that wasn't what Declan meant, nor did she plan to reveal that part of her past yet. Her feelings for Declan were too raw.

'You know a lot about housekeepers? You've seduced plenty?' Chloe tried to keep the conversation light.

'Never. You're the first.' His voice rumbled up from beneath her ear and she snuggled closer. 'And I'm not sure I'd call it a seduction. More like a mutual explosion.'

He paused, as if waiting for her to say something but she kept her lips closed, afraid of what might slip out.

'Yes, I grew up with housekeepers, here and in the family home in Sydney. My grandparents had them too. Worthy women with aprons and no-nonsense attitudes.'

Declan's hand stroked her waist. 'You don't fit the mould, Chloe Daniels.'

She shrugged, trying to ignore the tremors raying out from his touch. 'Nevertheless, it's what I do.'

'Did you always want to keep house?'

Chloe shook her head. 'I never knew what I wanted. Except as a teenager when all I wanted was to rebel.'

'That's normal. I was only eighteen, wet behind the ears, when I broke out on my own rather than follow in any of the family businesses.'

'That sounds very…commendable.'

He shifted as if turning to watch her, though of course that was impossible. 'How did you rebel?'

Chloe smiled wistfully. Strange how good it felt to share her past with the man who'd had her on edge for ages. She wrapped her arm tighter round his chest and was rewarded with a throaty murmur of approval.

'I was on the other side of the railway tracks from you, literally. By twelve I'd joined a graffiti gang and spent most of my nights in back alleys and on deserted railway sidings wielding spray cans.'

Declan shook his head. 'You never cease to intrigue me. That's so far from the image you project.'

'Which is?'

His hand stroked her side and she shivered as waves of delicious pleasure spread from his touch.

'Competent, no nonsense, reliable.' His caress changed, slid up towards her breasts. 'Delectable, sexy...'

'Enough!' Chloe grabbed his marauding hand. Tempted as she was, every time she gave herself to him it felt as if she lost a little more of her precious self-possession.

'You must have given your parents a few grey hairs.'

'I didn't live with my parents. I was fostered out.' Her lips firmed on memories of being shunted between foster homes. Of the desperate uncertainty, the hope, fear and distress of yet another move when things didn't work out. She rarely spoke of her childhood.

'That must have been tough.'

She shrugged, remembering the pressure to fit in, to be cute and compliant, undemanding and above all helpful, no matter how stressful the new placement. It had been a struggle for a lanky kid with bright hair and freckles whose smart mouth had hidden desperate self-doubt.

'I got by. After school I got a job as a chamber maid in a hotel and from there sort of fell into housekeeping.'

No need to explain that was the only job she'd been able to get with her poor school results. She and school hadn't got on, not till right at the end when she'd been placed with her foster parents Ted and Martha. Then she'd begun to blossom under their loving kindness.

'How do you go from that to running a place like Carinya?'

Chloe paused. Her past and Declan's were so different. His, a success story from birth. Hers, almost the opposite, until Ted and Martha, and then Mark. Declan worked not because he needed the cash but because he loved the cut-and-thrust world of business. For her work was a necessity. She needed every cent of her generous wage to cover Ted's expensive private rehabilitation facility. Then one day, when she'd saved enough, she'd open a catering business.

'Hard work. I was determined to make a success of myself. Lots of training—I did so many hospitality and catering courses I could whip up a *cordon bleu* meal for twenty if you needed it. Or a multi-tiered wedding cake.'

She halted, her pulse hammering as nausea rose at the idea of organising a wedding breakfast for Declan and some society darling. She hurried on. 'And there was luck too.'

'Tell me.'

She looked up at him, trying to gauge his interest. His damaged face, so familiar to her now, still had the power to make her chest squeeze tight.

'Why? It's not particularly interesting.' Chloe wasn't used to talking about herself. Was she afraid telling him would reinforce the social chasm between them? Was she such a coward?

'I'm interested, Chloe.'

He pressed a kiss to her lips and something inside melted. The tension that had risen thinking of her disastrous childhood eased. Even her anxiety about this fragile new relationship ebbed in the face of the well-being she felt in Declan's embrace.

Was there anything more important now than sharing with him? Building on this closeness? She'd already laid herself open, letting him in. She needed the courage to go further. She shivered, acknowledging she wanted the chance to have him in her life, not just for a short fling.

'I was working at an upmarket hotel in Sydney when Damon Ives came to stay.'

'The actor?'

Chloe nodded, remembering the excitement among the staff when his visit had coincided with his first Oscar nomination. 'Yes. I was one of the staff rostered to look after his suite. He got to know me over the month he stayed and at the end he offered me a job.'

'Really?' The rhythmic stroke of Declan's hand stopped abruptly and she was sure she detected disapproval in his tone.

'Yes, really.' She stiffened. It wasn't the first time she'd encountered suspicion about her relationship with one of the country's most handsome and charismatic stars. 'And before you jump to conclusions, Declan Carstairs, let me say I impressed him with my willingness to help out when he needed extra assistance. That's all.' She didn't say more. Damon had a right to privacy.

She shuffled up onto her elbow so she could see Declan's face fully.

'Did I imply otherwise?' His brows rose.

'You wondered. I could hear it in your voice.'

His mouth quirked up at one side. 'A mind reader, are you, Chloe?'

'You made it pretty obvious.' Appalling how much that hurt. How easily Declan's words could wound her.

'Then I apologise.' He wrapped his warm hand around the back of her neck and pulled her down to him. 'Forgive me?' His lips brushed hers and her breath caught at the strength of her compulsion simply to sink into his arms.

Declan kissed the corner of her mouth, licked her bottom lip, and she shuddered. 'Please, Chloe?'

If he'd ordered she might have withstood him. As it was she surrendered with a sigh of pleasure.

But when his hands moved purposefully, one to her breast and the other to her bottom, she rolled away onto her side. Sex with Declan was wonderful, but what she really wanted was the comfort of being held close, sharing more than their bodies.

Was she crazy to believe this could lead somewhere?

'No?'

Her lips curved at the disappointment in his tone.

'Soon,' she promised. Despite her caution Chloe knew she couldn't resist him for long.

'Tell me about you,' she urged, wanting him to share with her as she had with him. She needed to know their intimacy was more than skin deep.

'Nothing to tell. My life's an open book.'

'Really?' She couldn't ignore a bubble of disappointment. 'Nothing at all you want to share?'

He shook his head. 'Unless you count the fact that I've been having x-rated daydreams about my housekeeper.'

Chloe stifled hurt at his blatant diversion. 'Is that so?' Her hand drifted to his face, stroking his cheek, the rough line of his scar. She reminded herself he was a man who kept his own counsel. Sharing wouldn't come easily to someone so self-contained. What had made him like that?

'Yes. She has this prim and proper voice that's a complete turn on. Just listening to her read out the notes of a meeting makes me hard with wanting.'

Suddenly he grabbed her hand and held it in his, palm flat against his scarred cheek.

'This really doesn't bother you?' The light-hearted tone disintegrated and for the first time there was an edge to Declan's voice that hinted at emotion.

'I told you it doesn't.' Her chest cramped as she read the confusion on his face. The desolation.

She'd wanted real. This was it. The accident had changed his life and his scars were the least of it.

'Do your injuries hurt very much?'

'No. Just a bit of stiffness and an occasional headache.'

Liar. Chloe had walked in on him more than once when he'd been struggling, his face tight with pain as he pushed himself to the limit with his rehab exercises.

A wellspring of emotion bubbled up, filling her with the need to comfort him and herself.

He'd lost so much. And she… She feared she'd lost the safe, peaceful world she'd built for herself now this frustrating, intriguing man had burst into her life.

She laid her head on his shoulder, wrapping her arm over him and her thigh across his legs, as if to protect him from the demons that plagued him.

Yet who would keep her safe now the defences she'd painstakingly constructed after Mark's death had been scoured away?

'Chloe?'

Declan felt her blink against his chest. Was that

moisture on his skin? Was she *crying*? The astonishing notion confounded him and stole his breath.

He couldn't remember anyone crying over him. He must be mistaken.

'Are you OK?' he asked, his voice rough.

'Never better.' She tightened her hold and he was hard put to concentrate on not responding physically.

'It must have been a terrible accident,' she murmured. 'For you *both* to have fallen from that cliff.'

Instantly Declan stiffened. Too often sympathy had been a ruse to elicit gory details of the tragedy that had taken Adrian's life.

Yet Chloe said no more, just held him close.

Perversely it was her silence, her refusal to ask, that loosened his tongue on a topic he never discussed. Or maybe it was the need finally to share—not just with anybody, but the woman he'd begun to care for.

He'd kept the truth of that day to himself. He'd held his friends at a distance since the accident. Even if he'd had family alive he wouldn't have burdened them with the knowledge of Adrian's despair. It was enough that Declan shouldered the guilt for not saving him.

'It *was* terrible,' he said finally, his voice scratchy,

dredged up from a throat raw with pain. 'Like a nightmare.'

Surely it had happened in slow motion? Adrian's words, his cutting of the rope... So slow Declan should have realised sooner what he'd had in mind. Should have been able to prevent...

His hold on her tightened, her soft warmth balm against the hammer blows of guilt.

'It was a hard climb,' he recalled. 'Too hard.' He should have guessed that after years of soft living in London Adrian hadn't been up to it, despite his assurances.

'Hindsight's a wonderful thing.'

Declan tensed. 'That's no absolution.'

'Do you need it?' Her whisper lifted the hair on his arms.

There could be no absolution. Thinking of that day made his gut burn with familiar, hellish guilt. Every day, every hour trapped in this closed off darkness, haunted him.

'I'm... I was the elder, the more experienced one.'

'And your brother always did what you told him?'

Declan's mouth curled at the thought of Adrian taking advice. He'd always had to find out for himself. He'd been almost as stubborn as their father, or Declan.

'That doesn't excuse—' He shook his head. 'When I looked down and saw where Adrian had fallen...'

Chloe snuggled closer, her body a living blanket that surprisingly shaved away a fraction of the keen edge of pain. Remembering was anguish, but it was almost bearable.

'You didn't fall together?'

'No. My brother fell. This...' he gestured to his eyes and ruined face '...came when I climbed down trying to get to him.' They said Adrian hadn't survived the fall, yet Declan should have been with his brother at the end.

'You did your best. That's all anyone could ask.' The words feathered his throat as she rose up to kiss him. Her nipples brushed his chest and his arms closed hungrily around her, tugging her tight into him.

Chloe was the only real, sane thing in his world. She was safe harbour against the nightmares and the screams of conscience and he clung to her desperately.

He'd let his brother die and still hadn't brought the woman responsible to justice. Maybe, if he could do that, it would be some recompense for his failure.

With Chloe in his arms, a warm, sweet bundle of femininity, the raw gash of pain eased to a dull ache.

Declan took her mouth hard, demanding a response he was almost afraid she wouldn't give. But, as if sensing his desperation, she melted into him, yielding as his fingers bit into soft flesh and he tumbled her onto her back.

She didn't protest as he pressed her into the mattress, kneed her legs open and pushed into her honeyed warmth.

She didn't complain even when, with no foreplay or gentleness, he thrust hard and sure, again and again, slipping deep into her beckoning heat. Instead she wrapped herself around him, drawing him close. She rocked with him in a primal, desperate rhythm that beat in his blood so hard it obliterated guilt and memory and blasted away everything but them: Declan and Chloe.

He woke slowly, disinclined to lose the soul-deep wellbeing that came from a sated body, a warm woman and a comfortable bed. Not just any woman. Chloe. His Chloe.

Declan's hands twitched as if to hold her longer, seeking the peace, comfort and ecstasy she'd brought.

Slowly Declan made himself slide away, knowing if he stayed he'd wake her, demanding more. She needed sleep.

He shook his head. He'd never known anything like the cataclysmic sex they shared. The intensity of each touch, each breath, each shattering climax that ripped him asunder yet, conversely, seemed to rebuild him stronger each time.

He wrapped a hand around the back of his neck, grimacing. He could tell himself blindness had its compensations: sharpening his other senses so physical delight took on a whole new meaning. But deep inside he knew the difference was Chloe.

She refused to let him sink completely into the well of guilt and pain. She dragged him towards the light, making him want more. Making him dare to hope.

He'd never felt dependent on a woman till now. Instead of it being a weakness, Declan knew his feelings for her made him stronger.

Beside him she slept on and his conscience stirred.

He'd been rough that last time, with no finesse. Yet she hadn't demurred, had simply clutched him close and ridden the wild surge of passion with him. Never, even in the throes of youthful exuberance, had he so lost control.

That worried him.

Better to get up now before he changed his mind about resisting temptation.

If he wasn't mistaken, the sun was out. He could feel it on his bare body as he swung his legs out of the bed. He could...

Declan froze, his sleep-slitted eyes opening in instinctive shock.

One deep breath. Another. He dragged them in, forcing air into lungs that threatened to collapse. His fingers clawed at the sheets till the blood throbbed in his veins.

Was this some trick? An illusion?

Or had the doctors been right?

He'd spent so long dismissing their hopes as a ruse to keep his spirits up; the chance they'd been right seemed impossible.

Yet there it was: a strip of light. He could see light. If he lifted his head it grew brighter, too bright for his long-dead eyes.

Hastily he lowered his gaze and there another shock awaited him: hardwood floor, rich with a century or more of polish. The hand-loomed rug in gold and black he'd purchased a decade ago on one of his first business trips to Asia. Bare legs, familiar, but for the wide scar that ridged one thigh.

He put one trembling hand to his leg, watching

his fingers clench on skin, feeling his grip tighten as if in proof that what he saw was real.

Almost he was afraid to shut his eyes in case it was a dream. Like those mornings early after the accident when each awakening was a blow, a new reminder that he couldn't see, no matter how vivid his night-time dreams.

Air hissed from his lungs as he forced his eyes shut. His heart pounded against his ribs with fear and dreadful hope.

Carefully he opened them and the shock of sight froze him anew.

He could see! Hazily, not perfectly, but he could see. For days he'd imagined hints of light but had passed that off as wishful thinking.

His whole body shook in reaction. Thoughts flew through his brain too fast and incoherent to grasp. It was momentous, astonishing. He needed a witness, someone to share it with. He needed Chloe. She'd be ecstatic. He knew the hopes and concern she hadn't been able to hide, despite her brisk attitude.

Declan swivelled, shoving aside the sheet as he turned to her, his mouth already forming the words.

They disintegrated on his tongue, elation turning to bitter disbelief in an instant. He gasped, his breath constricting in reaction to an unseen blow that bludgeoned his chest, crushing his ribs.

It couldn't be. With a super human effort he dragged a breath into oxygen-starved lungs.

Frantically his gaze roved the woman asleep on his bed. She lay turned towards him, oval face tinted with the delicate flush of a well-loved woman. Fine, pale brows arched over closed eyes. Her long eyelashes were tinted darker than her brows, fanning ivory and rose skin. Her lips were as full and lush as he'd expected, reddened now, as was the delicate flesh near her lips and at her throat from his kisses and the abrasion of his stubbled jaw.

Something hard lurched in his belly as he saw how he'd marked her skin, branding her with his possession.

His hands clawed at the sheet as he catalogued her straight nose, neat jaw and cloud of wavy hair, rose-gold and glowing with life.

Declan slammed shut his eyes, forcing away the queasiness that stirred.

It couldn't be. It was impossible.

Yet even before he opened his eyes again he knew it was.

One final look and he catapulted off the bed, backing away to stand in the shadows, the thrill

of restored vision eclipsed by the fact that he recognised this woman.

He'd seen her picture on Adrian's phone. Her
sexy, slumberous smile had haunted his dreams
for too long. Her identity had been a mystery he'd
determined to solve from the moment Adrian had
killed himself.

Chloe Daniels was his brother's girlfriend. The
one Declan's investigator had failed to locate. Not
surprising, as she wasn't a visitor to Carinya but
lived here.

His brother's woman.

His breath stalled and his chest cramped as a
leaden weight dropped through his belly. His flesh
chilled.

She'd targeted Adrian then dumped him when
she learned he'd lost his fortune. Declan had seen
first hand how her betrayal and desertion had
driven Adrian to suicide.

Nausea rose in his throat as he surveyed her
naked allure, his numbed mind fighting instinctive denial.

This wasn't happening. It wasn't real.

Chloe was *his*. She was special. What he felt for
her had even eclipsed the years of cynicism and
distrust engendered by a false paternity suit and a
scheming, avaricious ex-lover.

Chloe had taught him to trust again. She'd stood by him when he was vulnerable…

Most vulnerable.

Slowly his brain engaged. Nausea swirled anew and the world tilted as it all began to make sickening sense. Hadn't Adrian said she'd left him to find herself a rich man? Wasn't Declan one of the wealthiest men in Australia?

He braced himself against the wall, his belly churning.

Chloe had tangled up his feelings. She'd pushed aside a lifetime's doubts engendered by watching his parents' less-than-close union. For the first time Declan had actually welcomed the idea of a long term relationship.

He remembered Chloe's patience despite his churlish demands for privacy. Her tenderness, well beyond the demands of her job. Her determination. The way she'd insinuated herself into his life, even his dreams.

Declan shook his head against the voice inside that screamed she was genuine, that she cared for him.

The evidence couldn't be shut out. She'd made herself indispensable to him while he was weak and grieving. When his defences were down.

What sort of coincidence was it that the woman

who'd captured Adrian's heart then rejected him
had become Declan's lover? He'd given up believing in coincidence when a smarmy lawyer had
slapped him with a multi-million-dollar paternity
claim for a child who wasn't his.

Abruptly he stumbled from the room, lungs
labouring with each sawing breath. He needed
space and time to confront this new nightmare.
He couldn't think straight.

The only reality in Declan's world right now was
the sound of his illusions crashing around him.

CHAPTER EIGHT

CHLOE woke to the roar of a helicopter. It blasted her consciousness with a heavy thud-thud-thud reminiscent of how her pulse had thundered when she and Declan made love. Instinctively she reached for him, but the bed was empty. Her heart dipped.

The vibration of the chopper's blades was so close it must be on the estate. She opened her eyes. The sun was so high she guessed it was afternoon.

On a surge of frantic energy she shot out of bed, only to discover her legs wobbled like jelly after a long night's loving. The realisation shocked her. She'd never experienced anything like the night she'd spent with Declan. Not even in the first flush of her relationship with Mark had passion been so all-consuming.

Chloe shoved the disquieting thought aside and stumbled to her feet, hauling her wrap on.

'Declan?' No answer from the *en suite* bathroom. He must have gone down to see who was arriving.

She cringed at the thought of being caught naked, emerging from her boss's bed. Last night they hadn't been employer and employee. But nor had they spoken of where their changed relationship might lead.

Chloe wished he was here to reassure her. So she could read the tenderness in his touch. A tenderness that had delighted her and eased her nerves.

Last night had been the culmination of weeks of tension building like a storm head in a summer sky. Yet the depth of her feelings shocked her.

When Declan had revealed his injuries had come from trying to save his brother, her heart had cracked at such tragic waste and desperate loyalty. She'd wanted to hold him till all his wounds, physical and emotional, had healed.

Did she love him?

Her heart thudded so loud it blocked the roar of the chopper.

Chloe waited for panic to engulf her. Instead a sense of peace settled. Whatever this was, it was right.

Finally she remembered the need for clothes and moved. She was almost to the top of the stairs when movement out the window caught her eye.

The chopper was on the helipad beyond the tennis court. As she watched two men walked towards it, heads bent. One she didn't know. The other was unmistakeable—wide shoulders, wind-tousled black hair, imposing frame.

It was Declan in jeans and a dark shirt she'd laundered yesterday. His gait was clipped, uneven, as if his leg pained him more than usual.

Hot guilt stabbed her. Last night neither of them had made concessions for his injuries.

Then she realised Declan was getting aboard!

Her blood drained away. He was leaving? Chloe clutched at the window sill as she slumped in shock.

As morning-after etiquette, this was a killer. But then she had no experience of mornings after with any man but her husband. She shook her head, utterly bewildered, her stomach hollowing. *This couldn't be happening.*

Was she so easily dismissed? Had that tenderness, the closeness they'd slowly built, meant nothing? Was this how Declan behaved with all women once he'd had his fill?

Distress and mortification churned her insides.

At the last moment Declan paused and turned his head, almost as if he saw her. Chloe's heart leapt, then catapulted down as he climbed into the helicopter. A moment later it lifted off.

Chloe blinked, her hand pressed to her mouth. She couldn't believe it. Even if there was an emergency there'd been no need to leave without a word.

It had been Declan's choice.

His actions were a smack to the face, leaving her bereft, nursing shock and bewilderment.

Chloe stared numbly long after the helicopter had disappeared. She had the awful feeling that if she moved she'd shatter like discarded glass.

Some time later the phone rang. She jumped, pulled her robe tight and stumbled into Declan's room to take the call.

That meant confronting the wide, rumpled bed, the tray with the remains of their supper. The condom packet on the bedside table. The sight of it, empty and carelessly abandoned, jolted pain through her.

Eventually the shrill ringing forced her to move.

'Ms Daniels?'

Her knees gave way and she collapsed on the bed. Had she hoped it would be Declan?

'Yes?'

'Hi, this is Susie in Mr Carstairs' Sydney office.' She sounded young and bright, a millennium younger than Chloe felt.

'Yes?' Chloe's voice was odd—faded and hoarse.

'Mr Carstairs has instructed that Carinya be

closed for the next few months. The gardener will act as caretaker. He wants you in Sydney tomorrow.'

Chloe shoved the hair back from her face with a trembling hand. 'Why Sydney?'

'Mr Carstairs will base himself there for the next few months.' Was that excitement Chloe heard in the other woman's voice? She could just imagine the stir Declan made among female members of his staff.

On a hiss of indrawn breath Chloe pressed a hand to her chest. Was that what last night had been? Convenient sex with a willing, available employee? Yet, try as she might, she couldn't cast him as a sexual predator.

There had been much more to it than convenient sex. In the long, dark hours of loving, through the gentle caresses, the fierce hunger and the tentative sharing of words, she'd believed Declan experienced some of the magic she felt. Surely she couldn't have misunderstood?

'Ms Daniels? Are you there?'

'Sorry. I'm here.'

'Oh, good. Mr Carstairs wants you to take care of his apartment. You'll be based in Sydney till further notice.'

* * *

Two days later bewilderment had given way to fury. Two days without a sighting, even a phone call from Declan. All his instructions had come via his staff.

If well paid jobs weren't so hard to find, if she wasn't so desperate for the income to support Ted, Chloe might have handed in her notice.

Except she needed to see Declan again. Needed to know what had happened. Was he all right? Had something terrible happened?

He'd slammed into her quiet, contented life, torn it up by the roots and flung out of it again, leaving her seething yet bereft, hurting yet worried.

She needed to talk with him but that wouldn't happen any time soon.

An eager, excited crowd filled the huge, vaulted living space of his penthouse. The glittering throng was backlit by a stupendous view of Sydney Harbour Bridge and the white crests of the Opera House.

Glass doors to the landscaped roof-garden were open and guests spilled out to the lush, almost tropical haven. Tonight it was transformed into party central with a massive bar and candles floating in the long pool. The guests were glamorous and dressed to impress, wearing enough bling to sink a battleship.

She'd spotted celebrities enough to keep a gossip magazine in print for a year and there'd been paparazzi outside snapping shots as they had entered.

Thank goodness she'd changed. Instead of her usual skirt, blouse and sensible shoes, she wore a black dress and heels. Cheap jersey instead of silk. Simple rather than designer chic. Modest rather than sexy. But at least she didn't look totally out of place now she was forced into the role of reluctant hostess.

She smiled at the couple beside her who were extolling Declan Carstairs' business acumen and bit down on her own pithy assessment of his character. Two hours into his own party and he still hadn't showed.

Maybe his cavalier treatment of her wasn't unique.

Her jaw tightened and fire skirled in her blood. Yet still his behaviour didn't ring true with the man she'd come to know. That was the puzzle.

'Ms Daniels.' She found the manager of the catering team at her elbow, like herself dressed to blend with the guests. She read concern in his eyes.

Excusing herself, she turned towards him.

'We'll be out of champagne soon and the food's running low. There are at least fifty more guests than expected.'

Chloe nodded. She too had been surprised when guests had kept streaming in. And they wouldn't shift soon. Not when there was no host to call an end to what she knew from overheard conversation was a rare, must-attend event, a celebration in Declan Carstairs' private home.

Why had Declan decided to socialise on such a scale? It was unlike the man she'd known at Carinya. The reclusive man who'd treasured privacy.

The man she'd thought she knew.

The thought scoured a hollow ache inside.

'Your chef, he can have anything from the pantry, or bring in his own supplies, even if you have to wake people to get them. Mr Carstairs will cover the cost. As for the wine, there should be more delivered soon.'

At his questioning glance, she shrugged. 'The guests look like they're here for the duration. I ordered more a while ago.'

'Good thinking.' He smiled and she knew relief that she had an ally in this chattering mass of strangers. She'd kept herself busy these last days but she walked a knife edge, her nerves shot and her emotions a mess. Managing an A list party alone was the last thing she needed.

'Check what's delivered. If you think it's not enough, let me know.'

He nodded then looked over her shoulder. 'I think our host has arrived.'

Even as he spoke Chloe sensed it.

The hairs on the back of her neck rose and the bare skin of her shoulders tingled. Excitement rippled through the room. Heads turned. Women lifted hands to their hair and necklines.

Chloe swung around. There he was, devilishly charismatic in a dinner jacket and bow tie, dark hair cut ruthlessly short now. Heat suffused her and her heart hammered against her ribs.

He was all right, then. How often had she feared some terrible relapse? Relief made her knees wobble even as anger surged.

His formal clothes contrasted with the blatant masculine planes of his hard face and the disfiguring scar. Yet the latter accentuated rather than destroyed the character and compelling attraction of his features.

Chloe's breath disintegrated, her heartbeat accelerating to frantic. He looked debonair, powerful and innately dangerous, far beyond her league.

Yet the secret heat swirling low in her abdomen, the tight budding of her nipples, were proof her body knew his. It had been no dream.

'Declan!' A platinum blonde in a strapless dress of silver sequins planted a kiss on his lips. She didn't seem in a hurry to break contact. Nor did he.

Chloe's fingers curled into claws.

'Vanessa.' Chloe just caught the deep burr of his voice over the chatter of the crowd. 'It's good of you to come.' His arm closed around the blonde's waist and she snuggled up to him.

On Declan's other arm a brunette with the face of a Latin siren and a curvaceous body in fitted scarlet pouted at him. As Chloe watched, Declan introduced the two women, both of whom remained cuddled close to him.

The crowd pressed forward. Declan smiled and shook hands, chatting easily. Chloe watched, fascinated, seeing him so at home in this high octane environment that reeked of wealth, ambition and success.

She was so absorbed it took a moment to process what she saw: Declan reaching out to shake hands. Declan greeting people by name as they approached.

Declan could see.

The realisation slammed into her with a force that punched the air from her lungs all over again.

It was fantastic, so wonderful she could scarcely

believe it, but there was no mistaking the way he interacted with his guests.

She swayed and groped for support. Her hand clutched the sleeve of the catering manager.

In the same moment Declan raised his head, looking beyond a plump little man with his model-tall trophy wife, to stare straight across the vast space at Chloe.

As if he'd known she was watching.

As if he'd known exactly where she was.

Like those times before when he'd turned unerringly to her, sensing her presence though she hadn't said a word.

The reminder of that inexplicable link hit her anew. It weakened her knees and she staggered.

'Are you OK?'

Silently she nodded.

Across the room eyes dark as jet meshed with hers. A pulse of connection, an unseen wave radiating from Declan and devastating everything in its path, pinioned her.

His smile disappeared. His features tightened.

He didn't look like the man who'd cradled her in his arms.

He looked like a stranger.

'I'm fine,' she whispered, releasing her grip on the catering manager and dragging her gaze away from Declan. Her skin prickled clammily and there was a buzzing in her ears. She swayed again but reminded herself she'd never fainted in her life. She wasn't about to start.

'You check those supplies. I'll come to the kitchen soon to see how things are.'

The caterer turned away and Chloe drew a shaky breath, trying to calm rioting nerves. She was torn between anger at Declan's behaviour and a thrill of joy at his restored sight. But when? How? Why hadn't he told her?

The crash of shattering glass jerked her head around. Over near Declan people stepped back, looking down.

In the ensuing hush she heard that low, familiar voice. 'It's all right, Sophia. The staff will deal with it. That's what they're here for.'

Across the room Declan looked straight at Chloe, his gaze unreadable. Again she was caught, transfixed by the force of emotions tangling around her.

Then Declan lifted one eyebrow. It rode high and challenging, a clear sign of impatience. It wasn't a request for help, that look, but an imperious command.

Cold drenched Chloe as she met his demanding gaze. His words circled in her brain. *The staff*

will deal with it. That's what they're here for.
Nothing more.

Something inside her shut down. On auto-pilot, she grabbed some napkins and made her way through the crowd.

So that was it? The sum total of Declan's feelings for her? Valiantly she fought off nausea. Could she really have been so mistaken in him? So naïve?

He'd had the hots for his housekeeper but it was over. He had his sight back and could choose from the loveliest women in Sydney. Chloe was merely an insignificant employee again.

Anguish tore a gaping hole where her heart had been.

All this time she'd known he was proud, even arrogant, but she'd never believed him to be a low life.

Lips firm, she forced her head up, ignoring the slashing pain as she reached him. He couldn't know her heart smashed against her ribs or that her self-possession hung by a thread.

'I'm so sorry,' murmured the brunette at Declan's side. 'I knocked my glass and—'

'No need to apologise, Sophia. If I don't care about a broken glass, why should my staff?'

His gaze met Chloe's and heat blasted through her, that familiar burst of electricity. She saw

Declan's eyes widen, their expression waver. Then he turned abruptly, gathering Sophia's hands in his.

Shards of ice slid down Chloe's spine. Bewilderment and denial rocked her back on her heels. He'd felt it too—she'd read the shock of sizzling awareness in his eyes. But he'd turned from her as if it, she, meant nothing.

To have Declan treat her as if she didn't warrant acknowledgement almost felled her. Declan, the man who'd made her feel again.

Because of him she'd dared hope for something more than a life of routine and emotional seclusion. In her naiveté she'd once called that contentment, but Declan had made her see she'd been living a half life.

It had taken her family years of love and patient understanding to convince Chloe she was worth caring about. She'd fought hard to overcome self-doubt and build her sense of worth through hard work and education.

She was damned if she would let him dismiss her as nothing.

The only saving grace was that no one here knew her humiliation. To them she was simply an employee doing her job. Declan had done nothing untoward. It was only he and she who knew how devastating his behaviour was.

Last time they'd been together she'd been in his arms.

Chloe dropped to her knees, her head spinning. Wine stained the hardwood floor and the edge of a fine cream rug. Her hands were quick as she gathered shards of glass. But her eyes prickled and she couldn't stop blinking.

She was all kinds of fool for caring.

Before her, less than a metre away, were his polished, hand-crafted shoes, the best money could buy. Above her his voice, deep and mesmerising, entertained his audience just as if she wasn't crouched at his feet.

Memory struck her of the day they'd met and she'd knelt before him, clearing another broken glass. She'd been annoyed by his arrogant attitude, not knowing it was blindness that made him so prickly.

He wasn't blind now.

He had his life back.

This was the real Declan.

Chloe gritted her teeth on a purging wave of fury that for a moment blanked out pain. When finally she stood, heat stained her cheeks.

'Oh, your dress! I'm *so* sorry.'

It was the brunette, gesturing to what Chloe now realised was her damp skirt. She'd knelt in the stain and not noticed. She supposed she should be thankful she hadn't cut herself into the bargain.

'It's OK,' she murmured, casting a reassuring look at the other woman. 'It'll come out.' In the meantime changing would give her a chance to escape Declan's presence.

By three a.m. everyone had gone. She was alone in the penthouse. Except she'd seen the light under the door of Declan's study and knew he'd retired there.

Was he alone?

Chloe thought of the brunette plastered to his side as he'd said farewell to the other guests. She remembered the fine-grained leather sofa in the study, long enough even to accommodate Declan's tall frame. She pursed her lips. It was none of her business who he spent his time with.

It wasn't as if she wanted it to be her.

She wasn't masochistic. Once bitten…

Deftly she grabbed some glasses the caterers had missed and went to the kitchen. She didn't need to finish cleaning tonight, but it was pointless going to bed. She'd never sleep.

Chloe had her hands in warm water, cleaning crystal flutes, when her neck prickled. She paused, willing away the sensation of awareness and stirring excitement.

Instead of abating, the sensation grew. Her nipples drew tight as if responding to cold, but it wasn't cold she felt. It was heat, from the nape of her bent neck, over her bare arms and down.

She swivelled.

Declan lounged in the doorway, his shoulders almost filling the wide frame. The harsh kitchen light showed his scar, more livid than she remembered, slashing his firm cheek. His jacket was gone and the top buttons of his shirt were undone, revealing a hint of tanned flesh.

Chloe sagged against the sink, her hands sliding to the bench on either side for support. How could the sight of him still affect her? Faint hope stirred that he'd come to apologise. Yet what apology could he make?

'Yes, Mr Carstairs?' She was proud of her cool tone. She'd made a terrible mistake, but she told herself she'd get over it one day.

'We need to talk.' He straightened and entered the room. To Chloe's horror he kept coming till the space shrank around him. 'And what happened to "Declan"?'

'Clearly that's no longer appropriate.'

That damnable eyebrow climbed up, accentuating the saturnine cast of his face.

'Clearly?' he purred in that rich, rumbling tone that played havoc with her composure. It enraged her that she still responded to it.

Chloe straightened, her spine stiff as a steel girder. 'Oh come on, D——!' She heaved a deep breath and was disconcerted to see his gaze dip to the V of her wraparound dress. An instant later his jaw locked tight, his mouth grim.

She wanted to ask about his returned vision. Reach out to the man she remembered behind the stern visage.

Except now she realised that man had been a mirage. The real Declan was selfish and shallow. There was no other explanation for his behaviour.

'You've made your position abundantly clear,' she said. 'I didn't have to be Einstein to work it out. And you're right.' Pride supplied the words. 'We're employer and employee. Anything else was a mistake.'

Yet a bewildered, grieving part of her wanted to demand he explain, even hoped these last days had been a terrible misunderstanding.

He stopped so close she inhaled the spicy scent of his skin. A rolling tide of awareness washed through her, drawing her flesh tight.

'A mistake?' His brow puckered and for an instant he was all too familiar, the man who hid deep emotions and unspoken scars behind a brusque manner. She even thought she saw uncertainty flicker across his face.

Then Chloe caught the direction of her thoughts. When had Declan ever been uncertain? He didn't need an apologist. His actions spoke louder than words.

She shrugged. 'It shouldn't have happened and it won't be repeated.' Bravado hid wounds she refused to reveal.

'Why? Because you've set your sights on someone else?' The words bit like nails, hammered hard and fast. She sensed anger surge in him.

'What are you talking about?' She shook her head. 'Someone else?' The only man with whom she'd had anything like a private conversation was the caterer.

Her pulse raced. She couldn't cope with Declan so near. If he didn't go, she might fracture in front of him.

'What is it you need, Mr Carstairs?'

He stiffened, his face hardening. She told herself her tone was professionally cool, not insolent.

He stepped nearer, cramming her against the sink, but she refused to cower. Instead she met his dark look unflinchingly. *She* had done nothing wrong.

'You think this is all about what *I* need?' His eyes gleamed dangerously. Apprehension tingled in her veins but she stood straight. 'What about admitting what *you* need, Chloe?' His voice dropped to a ribbon of seduction that she despised at the same time she reacted to it. 'I've never known a woman as needy as you for what I can give her.'

Flame seared her cheeks and throat. She'd been abandoned, wanton with this man. She'd experienced passion such as she'd never known and she'd revelled in it.

She opened her mouth to say he'd been just as needy then clamped her lips. A slanging match wouldn't help.

'If there's nothing else, I'll get on with the washing up. It's late.' When he didn't move she added, 'I don't need or want anything from you.'

She reassured herself it was true. Or would be, if only he'd leave her alone.

Her hands had just sunk into the warm water when he gripped her shoulders and spun her round.

'That's a lie, Chloe. We both know it.' His voice was pure gravel as he loomed over her, his face taut. Suppressed emotion radiated from him in waves.

She opened her mouth to deny it when warm fingers settled over her right breast, sure, hard yet gentle as they cupped her. Shock stole the words from her mouth. His hand moved, caressing, squeezing, and her throat dried.

One touch and he evoked a longing she'd thought she'd evicted from her being. One tantalisingly erotic caress and her knees were jelly.

'No!' She clamped a wet hand around his wrist and tugged. Nothing happened. Nothing except she felt the pull and shift of muscle and tendon as he changed his hold, plucking at her budded nipple through the fabric of her dress. Heat coiled deep within.

'Don't lie. Not about *this*.' His voice thickened as he leaned in, undeterred by the hand she shoved against his chest. He bit the sensitive spot between her shoulder and neck and shudders of longing engulfed her. Even her anger and hurt couldn't prevent her response. Her head spun.

He kissed the spot then suckled it and her nerves shot to clamorous alert. 'You want me, you know you do.'

It wasn't him she fought but herself. How could that be?

This man had walked out on her, rejected her. She couldn't want him. She couldn't!

'No.' She shook her head, still pushing desperately against him. Or perhaps not so desperately. Why had her hand tightened against his shirt? Not to push back but to mould his warm muscle. 'I'm not available for a quick grope now your fancy friends have left. I'm not your bit on the side.'

'Ah, Chloe, you were never that. You were always…' He groaned and tightened his hold, feathering kisses at the corner of her mouth.

She had nowhere to turn or hide, caught between his unyielding frame and the sink. His strong thighs surrounded her. The ridge of his arousal pressed against her abdomen.

Had she stopped struggling?

Damp heat pooled between her legs as he slipped his hand beneath the V of her bodice and bra. The skin-on-skin contact was her undoing. She shuddered as he pinched her nipple then bent to suckle her other breast through the thin material.

'Declan.' It was supposed to be a protest, but her hoarse voice turned it into a plea.

This was wrong, wrong, wrong.

Yet it felt…

'Yes?' His mouth moved against hers again, his voice cajoling. He didn't kiss her fully, just skimmed her lips and moved on to nibble her ear. His other hand parted the discreet gap in her cross-over skirt, and an instant later his fingers were against damp silk at the apex of her thighs. He pressed close and she almost moaned.

'You like that, don't you, Chloe?' His voice was a whisper of seduction in her ear.

She shook her head, struggling to drag herself from the whirlpool of sensation and think.

He pressed close, body to body, erection to her needy centre. A jolt of response rocked her whole being.

'Tell me, Chloe. Tell me what you want.'

She heard the words through a fog of sensual pleasure and rising need. Incoherent warnings flitted by but she couldn't grasp them. Instead all the emotions she tried so hard to ignore rose to the surface.

'What do you want, Chloe?' He breathed the words against her mouth and she arched into him.

'You,' she whispered on a sob. 'I want you.'

Bliss beckoned. He surged close, his arousal hard against her, his hands hot and possessive.

Then suddenly he was gone. His big hand slipped from beneath her bra, the other from under the edge of her panties. Cool air brushed her skin and dazedly she realised he'd undone the tie of her dress so it hung open, revealing her bare skin and sensible underwear.

She lifted a hand, whether to pull the gaping edges together or to reach for him she didn't know. Instead his voice stopped her.

'No!' The raw denial cut straight through the fog of sensual awareness. 'That will never happen again.'

Glittering eyes raked her. Then he spun on his heel and marched from the room.

CHAPTER NINE

AIR. He needed air.

His lungs couldn't suck in enough oxygen.

Declan strode away, shoved open a door and catapulted out onto the roof garden.

His lungs pumped frantically and now, finally, searing air filled his chest. For a minute there he'd wondered if he'd black out from lack of oxygen.

It was fury, he assured himself. Disgust at the woman who'd betrayed Adrian, broken his brother's heart and left him so distraught he'd committed suicide.

Together they were responsible for Adrian's death. She for driving him to it and Declan for not preventing it. Guilt swarmed like ants over his burning flesh.

What greater betrayal of Adrian than to take Chloe into his bed? To grab at the happiness denied his brother?

Nausea churned in his belly.

Chloe had tried to play Declan for a fool, delib-

erately targeting him as a rich, easy mark with his
blindness and his grief. Hell! He'd been so gullible, wanting more from her than he'd wanted with
any woman.

Even when his own eyes had confirmed her identity he hadn't wanted to believe the worst, had
fought it with every fibre of his being. Till he'd
been hit with even more proof of her culpability.
Proof he couldn't ignore.

Yet still he desired her. He even—and it shamed
him to admit it—felt jealous he'd shared her with
Adrian.

Bile rose, nearly choking him. How low had he
sunk?

In shock he'd left Carinya, unable to face the
enormity of his disillusionment, or the woman who
had torn him in two. She made him yearn to believe the impossible—that it was all some terrible
mistake.

For the first time ever he'd run, he who tackled
every challenge head on. For two days he'd been
in meetings and medical appointments, confirm-
ing his restored vision should be permanent. But
in reality he'd avoided her. Because he didn't want
to face the moment she confirmed the truth with
her own admissions. Was he such a coward?

He scrubbed a hand over his face.

Despite the new proof against her he was torn. Part of him clung to the memory of the honest, lovely woman he'd been on the verge of falling for.

Just now in the kitchen, desperation had driven him. He hadn't been able to keep his hands off her. He'd wanted to take her sweet mouth with his and lose himself in her sinfully addictive body. He'd craved it so badly his hands still shook with the force of control he'd had to exert.

He wanted the woman he'd known at Carinya. The woman he could respect and even…love.

Love? He'd almost fallen lock, stock and barrel for a fantasy.

She'd turned her sights on him when she'd discovered Adrian had lost his money with the failure of his London business. How convenient that Declan, wealthier than Adrian had ever been, had come to Carinya. She'd no qualms about going from one brother to another.

Was that why she'd delayed her return to the house? Had she feared Adrian had told Declan about her?

He stalked to the pool, reefing open his shirt. He needed more than air. He needed a workout to exhaust himself and dull the knowledge he'd been weak, touching her again.

That weakness sickened him. The mere sight of

her tipped him over the edge and made a mockery of his guilt and her betrayal.

Declan tore his shirt off, his hands going to his trousers, ready to get naked and work off his frustrations in the pool. But the sight of the water brought him up short. Last time he'd swum, he'd surfaced and found Chloe.

He shuddered and dropped his hand. Suddenly the pool didn't hold the same allure. With each stroke the caress of silky water against his skin would remind him of her touch.

Even in basic black, without jewellery or designer flair, Chloe had stood out in the throng of pampered beauties. With her ivory skin and her rose-gold hair up in an elegant chignon, she'd caught his eye immediately.

Declan told himself she wasn't beautiful. It was just that he'd learned the silken texture of her skin and the lush softness of her body.

Tonight he'd almost lost it when he'd seen her cosying up to a stranger.

When she'd knelt at his feet, so briskly competent, obviously unmoved by seeing him again, he'd wanted to lose the women he'd gathered close as protection against her, against the urge to stalk across the room and grab her. He'd wanted to haul her to him and brand her as his even while he'd wanted to shake her for daring to touch another man.

He'd stood, transfixed by the tiny, unexpected sprinkle of freckles across her nose and cheeks that made her appear almost innocent.

Innocent! He stalked across the garden, impatient at his own weakness.

He'd gone to the kitchen because his conscience demanded he face her at last. But the sight of her in that dress, held together with a single tie, its soft fabric outlining every dip and curve, had got the better of him.

'What the hell was that about?'

Declan shoved his hands into his trouser pockets as her husky voice shivered across the bare skin of his torso.

Slowly he turned his back on the city view, pushing away a moment's reluctant admiration that she was no coward. She'd followed him almost immediately.

She stood a couple of metres away, her chin lifted. Her hair was up but softened by delicate wisps that framed her face. Her dress was knotted tight, too tight, given the way it stretched across her breasts.

Heat dived in his groin and he firmed his jaw. He was too savvy to be fooled by that trick again.

'I *said*—'

'I heard you the first time.' He shrugged and watched with satisfaction as her narrowed eyes widened and dropped to his bare chest.

Deliberately he crossed one foot over the other and spread his arms wide on the railing, projecting a nonchalance he didn't feel.

Her mouth sagged before she remembered to snap it shut. He'd never been one for an idle life, but in these last months the long hours of exercise in the pool had toned his muscles even more. Almost enough, it seemed to make up for the ravaged face that stared back from the mirror each day.

People winced when they saw him, averting their eyes. But that hadn't stopped women tonight latching on to him. They loved his money and power.

Had Chloe shut her eyes rather than look at him when she'd shared his bed? Distaste curdled his belly and soured his tongue.

He should have been prepared for the fact Chloe's care and attention was mercenary. Yet it hurt. He'd truly *believed*.

'Are you going to explain yourself?' Her voice was jerky, as if she had trouble keeping her breath under control.

'I thought my meaning was clear.' He spoke

slowly, finding this harder than he'd expected. 'I wouldn't touch you even if you were sprawled naked in my bed.'

Yet, even as he said it, shuddering doubt undermined him. He watched her lush mouth firm and remembered the graze of her lips, hot against his skin. He remembered the way she'd knelt at his feet tonight and how it wasn't just the unexpected sight of delicate freckles that had held him rigid. It was the idea of her leaning in and…

'Why, because I dared to cross the line and stopped behaving as an employee?' He watched her wrap her arms around herself, as if cold despite the balmy night. Yet her chin stayed high, her eyes flashing. 'Don't tell me you have one rule for women and another for yourself? Once you've had a woman, you don't respect her. Is that it?'

He almost thought he discerned vulnerability in her face. Did he imagine that sexy mouth trembled? A rush of heat filled him and he leaned towards her. No, it was impossible. She was simply projecting emotion.

'Hardly.' He breathed deep. 'I like women. I just don't like you.'

Her jaw tightened as if he'd struck her. The pulse at the base of her throat trembled. He'd almost swear she paled.

He felt no satisfaction, only the desire to blurt out an apology. What sort of champion did that make him of his brother's cause?

'The feeling's mutual.' The words clipped out, sharp and precise from that lovely mouth. 'I've never met a more arrogant, rude man without even the most common courtesy.' She stopped and hefted in a breath that lifted her breasts towards him.

Declan kept his gaze fixed on her face.

'You're complaining about my *manners*?'

To his surprise Chloe stepped closer, her hands fisting on her hips. 'What *is* it with you, Declan? You think you can walk all over me? Nothing gives you the right to speak to me the way you have! Even if you've lost interest in me now you've got your sight back.'

'Oh, please, spare me the outraged innocence.' She must know by now he'd recognised her.

He watched one hand snap up towards him then stop abruptly, as if at the last minute she'd thought better of striking him.

Strangely, he'd almost have welcomed the slap. Punishment, not for his rudeness but for his weakness in still craving this woman.

He exhaled slowly. 'I know about you and Adrian.'

If he'd had any last, lingering doubts about Chloe's innocence, her instantaneous reaction banished them. Pale skin turned bone-white. Her eyes grew huge and her gasp was unmissable in the silence throbbing between them.

Disappointment swamped him. Had he really hoped she'd be able to explain away what she'd done?

Roiling emotion filled him. He had to force himself to stand still and face what he must. He owed Adrian, and himself.

'What do you know about Adrian?' Somehow she dredged the words from a throat shredded raw by the tears she'd fought back in the kitchen. Tears of fury and outrage, of self disgust and bitter, soul deep disappointment with the man who'd shown his true colours tonight. She'd hoped...

No! She couldn't go there. She couldn't face her naiveté in spinning hopes and dreams about him. She'd given so much of herself. Declan had merely enjoyed sex.

'I know everything.'

Stunned, Chloe looked up to find him standing closer, his feet wide and his arms crossed over his bare chest in a stance that signalled pure male domination.

A sensible woman would retreat but her feet were

rooted to the ground. She felt punch drunk, hit by so many conflicting emotions it was hard to think.

How did he know about Adrian? Had Adrian confessed his behaviour? If so, why mention it only now?

'Adrian…spoke to you?' She frowned, finding it hard to believe he'd confided in anyone.

She'd urged Adrian to talk with someone, anyone, knowing he needed help. Help she'd been unqualified to give, especially given the role in which his increasingly delusional mind had cast her.

Adrian had been ill. He'd refused to listen and had become aggressive if she pushed. He'd seen every attempt to guide him towards help as betrayal.

'You don't deny knowing him?' Declan pounced.

'Of course not. He stayed at Carinya after he returned from the UK. While you were in China. You know that.'

'Yet you don't talk about him.' Slowly Chloe shook her head, still disorientated by the change of topic.

She'd decided before she returned to Carinya that there was no point dredging up the harrowing past. There was nothing to be gained by mentioning Adrian's fixation except distress for her and his brother.

Now Declan claimed to know about it. Chloe frowned. 'What do you want me to say? What *is* there to say?'

'How about saying sorry? That would be a start.'

She gazed up at his tight-lipped face, feeling she'd stepped into a parallel universe where nothing made sense. Why were they talking about Adrian and not what had happened between *them*?

'I've already said I was sorry to hear he'd died.' But from the look on Declan's face, he didn't believe her.

His nostrils flared, his jaw hardened and his hand shot out as if to grab her arm. Then it dropped to clench at his side. Silence engulfed them, broken only by the thud of her pulse in her ears.

'You're denying your role in what happened? You don't feel *any* guilt?' Declan drew a breath that shuddered through his massive chest.

Chloe watched, bemused. She put a hand to her brow, pushing back wisps of hair that feathered her face.

'What do you mean? I didn't do anything to him.'

'Oh, you're good. Very good.' Declan's words burst out like machine gun fire. 'You look the picture of innocence.'

'I had no role in his death. You know that. It was a climbing accident.'

He thrust his head forward, invading her space.

'It wasn't an accident.' A shudder rippled across his skin. 'He killed himself. Killed himself because of you.'

His accusing finger pointed directly at Chloe. Her heart spasmed and she gasped, pressing the heel of her hand to her chest.

'No. That's not true. It couldn't be.'

But Declan merely stared back, his face cast in harsh lines. Chloe waited for him to recant and say it was a lie, but he didn't.

Slowly, like dank, creeping fog, awful doubt filled her.

She recalled how Adrian's friendly interest had changed to stalking, the continual invasion of her personal space. Finally she'd been unable to stay at Carinya. With his brother overseas, there'd been no one to make Adrian see reason or force him to seek counselling. No one except her, and every time she'd tried he'd accused her of betrayal, of not loving him as he did her. She shivered.

Could he really have been so deluded by his fantasy world that he'd taken his life?

'Tell me it's not true,' she pleaded, her hands twisting. 'Please, Declan.'

For what seemed an age Declan stared back, his

face eerily blank. When he spoke again his voice was devoid of inflection.

'We fell together but we were secured by a rope. Eventually I'd have found a way to get us back to safety.'

He paused, blinked, and then went on. 'He'd already shown me your photo. He'd described you in loving detail.' Declan's voice dripped acid. 'He raved about the wonderful woman in his life. How much you meant to him. How perfect your relationship was.'

Chloe reared back in instinctive denial, but Declan's hand shot out and grabbed her arm. His fingers burned like ice on her bare flesh, a living, unbreakable manacle.

'The day we climbed he was…different. Edgy, not so buoyant. And then, with the accident, it all came out. The truth he'd avoided telling me—how you'd betrayed him.'

Declan's hold firmed. 'How you'd used him then rejected him.' He grasped her other arm and leaned close, forcing her to bow backwards.

'How Adrian believed his life wasn't worth living without *you*.' Another tremor racked Declan's big frame and echoed through her.

'That's when he deliberately cut the rope and fell to the valley floor.'

A sharp cry pierced the air but Chloe barely recognised it as hers. Her mind was filled with the image Declan painted, of the troubled man she'd known falling down those endless cliffs.

Because of *her*, Declan had said.

It was nonsense.

It wasn't her fault.

Yet she felt herself shrivel and hollow with the terrible suspicion that perhaps, if she'd done more, it would never have happened.

She'd thought about putting in a harassment complaint with her employer but assumed, since the complaint was about her employer's brother, she'd simply lose her job.

She'd considered going to the police for a restraining order but had shied from such drastic action. After all, he hadn't actually hurt her.

She'd been a coward.

If she'd forced Adrian's increasingly unhinged mental state into the open maybe someone could have prevented his death.

Her blood froze.

The Adrian she'd met had been a loner, cut off from his London friends and in no hurry to re-establish himself socially in Australia. His brother had been busy overseas and Adrian was content to spend his time at Carinya.

Was she the only one who'd seen his descent into delusion? Who else had there been to witness it?

Guilt filled her. Had she done wrong in running that day he'd gone too far?

No. She might regret not reporting Adrian's actions, but she couldn't hold herself responsible for the fantasy relationship in his head. Once she'd left Carinya and heard the news of Ted's stroke, she'd put everything aside except the need to be with her beloved foster father.

It was regrettable, but it wasn't her fault.

It only felt like it.

Bruising hands still held her. Reluctantly she looked up into a face drawn sharp with grief and desolation. Did he hate her? Who could blame him when he thought she'd driven his brother to suicide?

'Let me go, Declan.' Her voice was heavy. 'You're hurting.'

Immediately his grip eased and she felt the brush of fingers on skin as his hands dropped. But he didn't step away, just loomed over her, his face a stiff mask.

She drew a deep breath. 'I need to explain—'

'You think I'd believe your explanations? You had weeks to tell me the truth yet you kept silent.' He turned his back and strode to the balustrade.

He stood silhouetted by the city lights, arms spread wide and bare shoulders hunched. 'Your explanations won't bring him back.'

The stark despair in Declan's voice stopped Chloe even as she started forward. What she had to tell him about his brother would bring pain. Yet she couldn't let him believe she was to blame.

'Declan, it wasn't like you think.'

His bark of laughter ripped the night air apart.

'You believe I'm that gullible, Chloe? I know you for what you are.'

She took a step closer, torn between distress at his grief and the need to set the record straight.

Because even now she harboured some fragile belief that what she and Declan had shared was special?

'Your brother and I didn't have that sort of relationship.'

She watched the bunch and play of muscles in his back and shoulders as he flung his head back, as if taking in the smattering of stars half-obscured by city lights.

'You say he lied?' Disbelief and weariness edged his tone, reminding her he'd already gone through too much.

'He told you…his version of the truth.'

Was there an easy way to tell a grieving man his lost brother had been mentally unhinged?

'Your brother misinterpreted—'

'No. Don't you dare tell me he misunderstood what was between you. I saw the photo on his phone. There was no mistaking that.'

Chloe gasped, her blood freezing as she recalled waking to find Adrian in her room at dawn, taking photos of her in bed. That was the morning she'd decided she couldn't go on pretending to cope.

Her heart galloped as she recalled Adrian's nonchalance, his belief he'd had every right to be in her room.

'It wasn't what it looked like.'

'No?' Declan didn't turn but his voice told her he didn't believe a word. 'You're telling me your relationship was platonic? I suppose you two never even kissed?'

Chloe hesitated, her tongue glued to the roof of her mouth. She'd never kissed Adrian but he'd kissed her, cornering her in the pantry. She'd shrugged him off, trying to make light of it. Perhaps that had been her first mis-step. Maybe if she'd shown how horrified she was, instead of trying to maintain a semblance of dignity, it would have nipped Adrian's interest in the bud.

'I suppose you never shared confidences either, you and my brother?'

Chloe recalled Adrian lingering in the kitchen as she baked, telling her stories of his life in London and his plans to rebuild his career. Before she realised how unhealthy his interest had grown, she'd shared her dream of establishing a catering business.

'We talked, but—'

'You talked. You kissed. And now, I suppose you'll tell me that photo wasn't of you in bed.'

'It was!' she burst out. 'But not with my permission. Your brother had no right.'

'No right to expect loyalty from his lover?' Declan turned and skewered her with a stare so fierce it dried the protest in her throat.

If he believed that, why hadn't he sacked her? Why wait till now to mention it?

'It's funny,' he murmured. 'When I saw your picture I thought my brother a lucky man. I changed my mind when I learned how shallow and mercenary you were. But when I saw you in the flesh that first time, I understood the attraction.'

'The first time?' The words strangled in her throat. Surely the first time was tonight.

'At Carinya.'

'You knew…then?' She frowned, her brain whirling.

'I knew then.' His voice held a heavy, lifeless quality that twisted her heart. Till she read the contempt in his dark eyes that once had blazed with tenderness.

Pain scoured deep, radiating in all directions.

'You believed I'd betrayed your brother and yet you slept with me?' Her hand crept to her mouth in horror.

It couldn't be true. It couldn't.

Something flickered in his eyes, something Chloe couldn't read. Finally he shrugged, the movement jerky.

'There wasn't much sleeping involved.' He paused, as if gathering himself. 'Besides, I needed to be sure.'

Her gasp shattered the silence. Nausea rose.

No wonder he'd given off mixed signals that night, pushing her away and taunting her even as he'd drawn her to him with his charisma and potent sex appeal. He'd known she wore silk and talked about how she looked.

How had she not known? She'd thought that night had meant something to him, as it had to her.

Chloe swayed and stumbled back. She squeezed

her eyes shut for a moment, trying to stop the world spinning.

Out of the corner of her eye she caught a blur of movement, as if he reached out to steady her. But he didn't touch her. She must have imagined it.

'Sure about what?' Was that thread of sound her voice?

When she looked again his expression was un-readable.

'Sure you were the sort of woman who'd blithely betray my brother when a better opportunity came along. That's what I was to you, wasn't I, Chloe—a better opportunity? You had no qualms about sleeping with both the Carstairs brothers for what you could get out of it.'

She stood rooted to the spot, telling herself she wasn't hearing this. Her head spun dizzily.

'It was necessary.' Declan surveyed her as if he read and understood every tiny, tell tale reaction of her body. 'But not without some compensations.'

Her heart jerked hard against her ribcage as her hand smacked his cheek.

He didn't even flinch.

CHAPTER TEN

DECLAN strode down the corridor, ignoring the aromatic scent of coffee that teased his nostrils. He didn't want to face Chloe this morning.

Last night he'd confronted her with the truth and she'd had no answer for it. He hadn't felt vindicated or triumphant. He'd been gutted.

The hot imprint of her palm against his cheek had briefly raised his hopes that the real Chloe, the one he'd fallen for, was back. But the hope had been short-lived. She'd had no answer, no explanation. No excuse. He had to face the fact that the real Chloe was the one who'd seduced both his brother and himself in the hope of financial gain.

Yet the memory of her hurrying away last night, one hand pressed to her mouth, evoked guilt. As when he'd let her believe he'd slept with her as a test of her character and greed.

He'd lied.

Declan firmed his jaw. Pain had made him lash out, capitalising on her misunderstanding. He wasn't proud of what he'd done. He'd almost re-canted in the face of her stricken look.

Till he'd remembered Adrian's anguish. Whatever Chloe felt was nothing to what she'd in-flicted on his brother. Yet still he felt torn between what he owed Adrian and what he felt for Chloe.

Declan had worked it all out now. Adrian's men-tion in his note of her dumping him for a better prospect had been written just days before Declan arrived at Carinya. Why stick with the bankrupt when the other Carstairs brother was a billionaire?

He recalled how Damon Ives had offered her a job after they'd met in the hotel where she'd worked. It seemed all too likely she'd slept her way into the job.

She said she'd never had money. Had she been so poor, so desperate, she'd sell herself for a little luxury?

He dragged his fingers through his hair. Surely he wasn't finding excuses for her?

'Declan.' Chloe's voice, thrumming low across his senses, pulled him up.

She stood in the doorway: crisp white shirt, straight grey skirt and sensible shoes. Hair pulled back and hands clasped at her waist. A hint of white, flour perhaps, on one cheek, as if she'd been industrious in the kitchen. It added authenticity to her wholesome image.

If her face looked too pale, so those tiny freckles stood out on her cheeks and neat nose, he told himself it was the sign of a guilty conscience. That must also be the reason for the smudges beneath her eyes.

Yet Declan had to shove his hands in his pockets lest he be tempted to reach out and smooth the tiny frown pleating her brow.

'We need to talk.' Her jaw angled defiantly. The gleam in her eyes snared him and he found himself leaning closer.

Abruptly he straightened.

'Very well.' He turned and led the way to his study. She was right. They hadn't finished this.

'I've made cinnamon rolls and coffee in the kitchen.'

So she *had* been baking. Now she mentioned it, a sweet, yeasty fragrance mingled with the beckoning scent of coffee. Had she hoped to win him over with her cooking?

Lips compressing, he took his seat behind the vast desk. She entered slowly. Was she disappointed he didn't take up her invitation for a cosy kitchen chat?

He leaned back in his chair, steepling his fingers. 'You wanted to speak with me?'

Her pale eyebrows rose a fraction but she looked calm, her spine erect.

'I need to tell you the truth about your brother and me.'

Declan's heart lurched to a faster beat. He told himself it was anticipation he felt, yet the last thing he wanted was to hear about Chloe and Adrian together.

'You weren't in the mood to listen last night and I...' Her gaze darted towards the doors leading to the roof terrace. 'I found it difficult coping with so many revelations.'

He said nothing.

She turned and suddenly he found himself drowning in remarkable apple-green eyes. It was hard to believe anyone with eyes the colour of spring and innocence could be so culpable.

He'd been gullible. For the first time in his life, he'd truly opened himself to a woman—not as a short-term lover, but as something more. He'd wanted...everything with Chloe.

Silently he cursed himself for wishing even now the truth could be different.

'At first Adrian didn't have much to do with me.

After all, I was the hired help.' Her mouth twisted as if in wry amusement.

Declan stiffened. He didn't want to know details of their journey into intimacy. But if that was part of his punishment for letting Adrian down, he'd force himself to listen.

'But he didn't seem to have anyone else to talk to.'

Familiar regret shot through Declan. If he'd known Adrian was troubled he'd have dropped everything to be there on his brother's return from the UK. But Ade had assured him he was fine and ready to enjoy some R and R.

'He had friends,' Declan said, assuring himself as much as her. 'Adrian grew up with a wide social circle.' It was unavoidable, given their parents' active social lives before their untimely deaths.

Chloe lifted her shoulders. 'All I know is that he kept to himself. The people he spoke about were those he'd left in London, like his business partner, Diana. He talked of her all the time.'

'And you decided it was your duty to keep him company, because he was lonely?'

Chloe didn't react. Her face remained smooth of expression, unnaturally so.

'Tell me about him.' Declan was hungry for anything that would help explain Adrian's depression.

Even now it didn't seem real. There'd been no hint of mental illness in their phone calls and emails, though he'd seemed more preoccupied than usual. Declan had put that down to natural concern over his bankruptcy.

Again her gaze shifted. 'He couldn't seem to relax. As the days passed he became restless, almost agitated.' She paused and Declan sensed her tension. Was it because she'd realised he wouldn't let her off the hook easily?

'He sought me out more and more.'

Declan swallowed a sharp retort. Had Adrian sought her out or had she pursued him?

She must have seen the disbelief on his face. Her eyes glittered and her jaw angled infinitesimally higher.

'It's true. He talked about his schemes for turning his business around and how good things were going to be when he pulled off some big business coup he was planning.'

Declan frowned. That didn't make sense. Adrian's business had gone bankrupt. Declan had had to assist his brother financially the last several months. There was no way Adrian's business could have been salvaged. Adrian had admitted to Declan he wasn't sure if he'd even go back to advertising or take up Declan's offer of a job.

As for him sharing his financial situation with Chloe—according to Adrian's note, that was when she'd dumped him.

'But it was more than that,' she continued. 'He *changed*. It seemed whenever I entered a room, he was there. He'd just…watch me go about my tasks.'

Did he imagine a tremor in her voice? 'What do you mean? He went out less so you saw more of him?'

Again Declan berated himself for not being there.

'That too.' She wrapped an arm around her waist. Emotion stirred at the sight of her apparent vulnerability but he thrust it aside. 'Mainly it seemed he anticipated my movements. Everywhere I went he'd be there, waiting.' Her words quickened. 'He even followed me when I went out. Then he'd question me about anyone I met or spoke to, as if he were jealous. It was…not normal.'

Declan sat up straight, his hands wrapping tight on the arms of his chair as precognition prickled his spine.

She couldn't be saying what he thought she was saying.

'You're telling me Adrian stalked you? That's preposterous!' The knot of inner tension combusted into indignation. How dared she say such a thing about Adrian?

Declan *knew* his kid brother. He'd virtually raised him since their parents had been immersed in business and social activities. Ade had been a great guy, without a malicious or devious bone in his body. He wasn't a stalker.

'You're maligning him because he's not here to defend himself.'

'I'm telling you the truth.'

Declan scoured his stunned mind for words. 'You ask me to believe he developed an *obsession* with you without any encouragement?'

Everything in him rejected the idea. Not Adrian. Not the brother he'd loved.

Despite his anger, Declan had been ready to consider there might have been extenuating circumstances prompting Chloe's action. That surely she wasn't the mercenary witch the evidence painted her. But with this allegation she'd gone too far.

'He did.' She met his disbelieving stare unblinkingly. 'I gave no encouragement except that I listened. But suddenly he was talking about us as if we were a couple, with a history between us. As if we were lovers.'

'And you weren't lovers?' Just thinking of it made his stomach curdle.

Chloe shook her head. 'We weren't. He wasn't my type.'

Declan heard a catch in her voice as if she found it hard to speak over welling emotion.

Then he remembered Adrian, just before he died, describing how she'd dumped him to go after someone with more money. He recalled how Chloe had decided he, Declan—disfigured, antisocial and brusque to the point of rudeness—*was* her type. How eagerly she'd given herself to him even when, after months of celibacy, he'd forgotten how to be gentle with a woman.

What could she have seen in him then but access to his wealth and an easy lifestyle? Just as years before an ex-lover had seen him as a shortcut to a pampered life.

He shied from remembering how much Chloe had meant to him in those dark days. It had all been a sham. The fact that even now he longed for the woman he'd known then made the anger and self-contempt in his belly burn hotter.

Torn between believing in the brother he'd known and loved for a lifetime and the woman he'd fallen for in a few short weeks, how could Declan even hesitate? He'd already failed Ade once. His shoulders slumped as a leaden weight settled in his belly.

His brother had never had trouble attracting women. Nor had he been a liar. Adrian wasn't a predator. He'd *never* have stalked a woman.

But then Declan hadn't realised Adrian was prepared to kill himself, had he? The damning voice in his head made him frown.

'He spoke of places we'd been together.' Chloe's creamy complexion flushed. 'He got angry when I didn't know what he was talking about and accused me of wanting to break off our relationship to take up with someone else.' She bit her lip.

'If my brother was bothering you, why didn't you report him?'

'I thought of it. I almost went to the police, but it was my word against his. Besides, he had a right to be in your house.' She looked away. 'But finally he frightened me. He was encroaching more and more and I thought—'

'Yes?'

'I worried about what he might do. There were days when he seemed almost normal but more when I thought he might act on his beliefs.'

'Force you, you mean?' Declan's blood congealed.

She spread her hands, her gaze skimming away. 'I don't know. I just felt scared. That was why I left.'

'You went because of a family emergency. That was what you told my personnel department.'

'It's true.' She paused. 'Well, I didn't leave because of that. I left because of Adr… Your brother. But I'd no sooner got away than I discovered my foster father had had a stroke. I used the leave to be with him.'

'Quite a coincidence.' And very convenient.

Her gaze shot to his and energy jolted through him. He hated that she could do that to him still.

'I suppose it is. But, believe me, I'd rather neither of those things had happened.'

Declan clenched his hands. 'And your foster father?' If there *was* a foster father. Once he'd have believed unhesitatingly. Now he'd check.

'He's in a private rehabilitation facility.'

'I suppose he can vouch for what you say?'

'No.' Her posture wilted. 'I didn't want to worry him.'

'But when he was getting better, surely you'd share your experiences with someone so close?' He paused, watching her intently. 'Unless you have some other *intimate* friend for that.'

Something disturbingly like jealousy jabbed him.

'It was all over,' she said flatly. 'Your brother was dead and I saw no point worrying Ted by raking over what was finished.'

Finished because Adrian had plunged to his death.

Because Declan had failed him.

Because Chloe had driven him to it.

She sounded plausible. That stoic posture and hint of a trembling lip spoke to the inner man who still, despite everything, yearned to cherish and protect the woman he'd believed in.

But Declan couldn't take her word for this. She forgot he *knew* his brother. She'd had all night to come up with a story, and that was all this was—a story to gloss over her role in his death.

'If you didn't go to the police, did you tell my people? My staff members have a right to safety at work.'

Her lips drew up in a pained smile. 'I was afraid I'd lose my job if I made a complaint about your brother. Good jobs aren't easy to find.'

'I see.' A convenient excuse. 'So you have no proof. It's your word against Adrian's reputation.' Disappointment filled him that she'd invent such a story. 'How does it feel, tarnishing a man's character when he can't defend himself?'

Scarlet slashed high across her cheekbones. 'It's not like that.'

She looked the image of innocent outrage.

Yet Declan had learned long ago that people

weren't always what they seemed. Growing up with wealth, he'd discovered some would do anything for a fraction of what he had. A pity he'd forgotten that when he met Chloe.

'You ask me to believe by brother killed himself for love of a woman he barely knew? That he *imagined* the great love affair that had transformed his life?'

The colour leached from her cheeks. 'It's not so unbelievable. Some men become obsessed with women they barely know or have only seen in photos. They build up a fantasy that's more satisfying than reality.'

Declan shoved his chair back from the desk and shot to his feet, unable to sit while she slandered Adrian.

'You're an authority on the subject?'

'Of course not. But I read—'

'Stop!' His voice reverberated around the panelled walls. 'I gave you a chance to explain, Chloe.' He shook his head. 'But I refuse to hear more lies.'

He'd failed Adrian once. He wouldn't do it again. Giving credence to this story would be a betrayal. The brother he'd known would never have threatened a woman.

'They're not lies.'

Wearily Declan unlocked a drawer in his desk

and dragged it open. His stomach clenched as he forced himself to reach in. A second later he slapped a slim black volume onto the desk.

'Then you can explain this.'

'What is it?' She eyed the book warily.

'Adrian's diary.' He watched her expression freeze. 'In it he details the time he spent with you. And there's a photo of the pair of you together at Echo Point.'

Declan shoved his hands into his pockets. He didn't like touching the book; it felt like trespassing. He'd read enough only to discover proof that Adrian and Chloe had been lovers—it was there in black and white—then he'd snapped it shut as nausea engulfed him.

When he'd left Chloe at Carinya his mind had been spinning, his emotions in a whirl. By the time he'd arrived in Sydney, he'd half talked himself into believing he'd been mistaken. Till Adrian's diary had killed all hope.

'Whatever he wrote wasn't true. As for the photo, he got a tourist to take it one day when he followed me out.'

Declan didn't answer. He turned on his heel and strode away, unable to stomach any more.

'Where did you get it? I don't remember seeing it.'

If she had, she'd have destroyed it. 'I found it the day after you left Carinya. I went back there.'

Foolishly he'd sought proof that he was wrong about her. Instead he'd found Ade's notebook locked in a bureau and with it heirloom jewellery their mother had bequeathed to Adrian. Had he withdrawn them from safekeeping to give to Chloe, to try to salvage their relationship?

Declan stared unseeing out the window. Everywhere he turned there was proof Chloe was everything he despised. He should be glad he'd learned the truth about her.

Yet he felt no relief.

Chloe stared at his broad back in that exquisitely tailored suit and felt the chasm between them yawn impossibly wide.

'Whatever's in the book is a product of your brother's imagination.' She had a sinking feeling she knew what sort of imaginings Adrian had written.

Declan swung around and her words died in her mouth. Morning sun lit one side of his ravaged face, highlighting the scar that today seemed a symbol of all the harsh emotion within. It matched perfectly the air of danger that clung to him and the martial light in his eyes.

Chloe remembered how it had been between

them, the growing rapport, the sharing and the excitement. The sense that whatever fragile filament spun them together was touched with magic, bringing emotions she'd never expected to feel again. Bringing hope and happiness.

It had been an illusion. Just like the shadow of anguish she thought she read now in his eyes. She blinked and it was gone.

In the stark Sydney sunshine, Chloe saw how ridiculous her hope had been.

She'd wanted to believe this was a mistake. That, despite what he'd said last night, Declan cared for her. That he lashed out now from shock and grief; confronting the truth about Adrian must be appallingly hard.

But she'd been wrong about Declan's feelings. He'd seduced her deliberately, unemotionally.

Pain lanced as if he'd used a knife on her.

What she'd imagined was mutual delight had been something tawdry.

Telling herself the man she'd fallen for was a mirage didn't help. Her stubborn heart couldn't take it in, as if, deep inside, she still believed what they'd shared was genuine.

'I'll never convince you, will I?' Abruptly anger was snuffed out by a sense of loss so great it reared up to engulf all else. Loss for what might have been and for the grief Declan still carried. This was a lose-lose situation, with both of them doomed to suffer.

Chloe wanted to reach for him, plead with him, *make* him believe. But his loyalty to his brother ran deep. Their relationship had spanned a lifetime. How could she expect to compete with that? He'd never take her word over his brother's. She'd known the truth would be difficult for him to accept. Now she realised it was impossible.

Declan's grief outweighed everything else. And she understood. Hadn't she spent months blaming hospital staff for Mark's death when the truth was no one could have saved him by the time he'd got there?

Declan needed someone to blame. Himself and her.

'No. You can't convince me.' His tone was lifeless, like her hopes.

'In that case I'll go.' Her shoulders slumped. 'There's no point me staying.' Money would be tight; she didn't know how she'd meet Ted's costs, but she'd find a way.

'No.'

His voice jerked her head up. 'Sorry?'

'You'll stay right where you are.'

She took a step towards him then halted, reading his grim expression.

'You don't want me here, Declan, and I don't want to work for a man who believes me a liar. Why prolong the bitterness?'

She spread her hands before her in unconscious appeal.

His lips twisted and for a heartbeat she thought she saw the man she'd fallen for—the one who hid his emotions behind a mask. Then he seemed to gather himself.

'And let you just walk away? You seduced Adrian when he was vulnerable after the loss of his business, made him fall for you then dumped him without a second thought.' He counted the accusations on his fingers.

'You knew he was depressed. I remember you talking so convincingly about your friend with depression. That was Adrian, wasn't it? But you didn't raise a hand to help him.' Another finger rose and her pulse thudded. For that, at least, she felt guilt.

'Then you turned your sights on me.' His eyes flashed. 'I was easy prey, wasn't I, Chloe? Blind. Alone. Sick with grief. A little judicious sympathy and—'

'It wasn't like that!' Chloe's heart broke anew that he could believe it of her.

'No?' One dark eyebrow shot up. 'You were so convincing, you even made me...'

Chloe held her breath as she waited for him to finish. Made him what? Care for her? Love her?

Foolish, hopeful woman.

'Was Adrian the first? Or did you start earlier with your *friend*, Damon Ives?'

Her breath hissed from lungs pinched tight in disbelief. Eventually she found her voice. No matter that pain made it wobble.

'Why do you want me here, Declan? For revenge? Is that it? To make me pay somehow?'

He didn't answer, simply watched her through narrowed eyes. Meeting his shadowed gaze, she sensed the pain he kept tightly shuttered. Her heart ached, but she couldn't help him.

She shook her head. 'This ends here.' Staying would be madness. 'I resign. I'll work out my notice and then I'll be gone.' Pride stiffened her spine and kept her voice even.

She refused to run as if she was guilty. Declan mightn't understand the significance, he was so mired in grief and denial, but it mattered to her. Pride was all she had left.

CHAPTER ELEVEN

'I'M SORRY, Chloe, but Mr Carstairs has changed his mind about tonight's dinner.'

At Susie's apologetic tone Chloe put down the whisk and bowl and shifted the phone that had been clamped between her ear and shoulder.

'You're joking.' Grimly she surveyed her preparations for an intimate dinner for two.

Declan entertained a different woman every night, reinforcing the huge chasm between Chloe and the accomplished, beautiful socialites he dated.

Steadfastly she'd concealed her hurt, telling herself it didn't matter. Yet working out her notice became harder each day. Nevertheless it was something she had to do, to show him he was wrong about her. As a kid she'd consistently lived down to expectations. It had taken years to convince herself of her own worth and she wouldn't relinquish that hard-fought achievement now.

She refused to run and have him see that as proof of her guilt. She'd leave with her head high.

'He's cancelled the dinner for two.' Susie paused. 'He wants something bigger. He said you'd have no trouble whipping up a *cordon bleu* meal for twenty. They'll arrive at seven-thirty'

Chloe looked at her watch and felt panic swell. It would be almost impossible to organise.

Then a wisp of memory surfaced that banished practical concerns. Of her telling Declan that night in bed that she could whip up anything from a gourmet dinner for twenty to a wedding cake.

He'd remembered *that*?

What else had he remembered?

She shivered and tried to push away memories. But that night was still emblazoned on her brain. Not just the ecstasy, but the wonderment, the emotional awakening and the sense of connection.

Yet for him it had only been a distorted test of her character. Did the tests continue? Lately he'd left large sums of money lying around. Was he distracted or did he hope to catch her stealing?

Indignation burned. She'd been a rebel as a kid but never a thief.

'He also wants you to act as hostess.'

'Sorry?'

'Mr Carstairs wants you to attend the dinner and help with his guests. And one more thing. He asked that you wear your green dress.' There was curiosity now in the secretary's tone. 'The one with the tie, he said.'

Heat fired under Chloe's skin as she remembered the party. The way Declan had seduced her with his touch. How the soft jersey dress had come apart in his hands and how close she'd been to coming apart too.

Shame scorched her and she cringed. It wasn't enough to set her the impossible task of preparing this dinner. Or that he kept her on tenterhooks wondering if he really was bent on revenge. He wanted to gloat too. She'd have to sit across from Declan, watching him watch her and knowing he remembered how completely she'd been at his mercy.

It was the final straw. She'd had enough.

Chloe's jaw firmed. She'd wear the dress. She'd show him she was completely immune to him now. Then she'd leave. She refused to stay, pining for a man who didn't exist.

Declan couldn't tear his eyes from Chloe, vibrant and enticing at the far end of the table.

She assumed he wanted her here to exact revenge. Yet nothing he did now could bring Adrian back.

Another man might keep her close to prevent her seducing some other guy for his money.

Though, strangely, his investigator hadn't found evidence of previous wealthy lovers. Only a long-dead husband, a teacher. That news had floored Declan. His visceral reaction, far too like jealousy for comfort, disturbed him.

He'd found himself wondering anew about the feisty yet caring woman he thought he'd understood at Carinya. He'd wanted to take the investigator's report at face value, proof of his own gut instinct that Chloe was that woman.

Till he remembered Adrian.

Guilt scored deep. Did he want to absolve Chloe for himself because he yearned still for the delicious, unique woman he'd known? What of Adrian, his grief and despair? How could Declan let himself believe in the woman who'd betrayed his brother so fatefully? It meant accepting Adrian had been a dangerous stalker who'd made a woman fear for her life. The idea was anathema.

Declan gulped a mouthful of wine.

Never had he felt like this, as if caught fast in quicksand that deepened whichever way he turned.

It was as well Chloe didn't know he wanted her here not for revenge, but because he couldn't let her go.

It shouldn't be so. Yet he yearned for her with a

desperation unlike anything he'd experienced. It tore him apart.

'Delicious rock lobster, Declan. Declan?'

He gathered his thoughts and found an encouraging smile for Sophia. She was exquisite in a fitted dress of beaded lilac and she hadn't stopped her engaging banter since the first course of what, he had to admit, was a superb meal.

Damn Chloe. Was there anything she wasn't up to? From dealing with impromptu parties, to fussy guests and requests at all hours, she'd proven herself a superb housekeeper. As if she really was what she seemed: hard-working, capable and with a skill for putting guests at ease. A skill he'd succumbed to in those dark days when loss and blindness had driven him to seek out her warmth.

Declan snapped his head up, cutting off that train of thought.

Chloe was far too sexy in that slinky green dress. His fingers tickled with the memory of how good she'd felt in it, and how much better she'd felt without it.

It had been a mistake to demand she wear it.

The slow burn in his blood flared hotter. He told himself the image she projected was a lie, yet doubts had crept into his certainty. Such as when he'd learned she did indeed have a foster father who'd recently suffered a massive stroke. Or when there'd been no tangible proof of rich lovers. The doubts turned each night into a restless trial as cold logic warred with the desire to trust.

His mouth tightened. He wasn't the only one drawn to Chloe. On either side of the table men leaned close, eager for her attention. But she played it cool, keeping a slight distance despite her friendly smile.

She was an expert at tantalising a man.

'I can manage on my own.' Chloe pasted on a perfunctory smile as she stopped at the kitchen door.

'Now, now.' Daniel wagged a finger as his gaze dropped to her breasts. 'Anyone would think you didn't like me.'

Chloe strove to unclench her teeth. Why, of all Declan's guests, did this lech have to follow her? 'I need to organise coffee—and,' she added with emphasis as his hand settled on her bare arm, 'I'll be quicker alone.'

He leaned in, his hot breath wine-laden. 'It would be a perfect time for us to get to know each other better, away from the crowd.'

'Let me go, Daniel. I didn't invite you to touch me.'

His blue eyes glittered as if her resistance fuelled

his determination. 'But that's what you want, isn't it, Chloe? That aloof air is a ploy.'

She stiffened. She'd had enough of men who thought they could speak for her or judge her. Men who saw only what they wanted. Declan at least had grief as his excuse; this vermin had none.

'I asked you to let go. I won't ask again.'

The warning had no effect. 'Don't think I haven't noticed the way our host looks at you from the other end of the table.' He winked. 'It's obvious you're far more than a housekeeper. At a guess I'd say you're very...*versatile*.'

His gaze trawled and Chloe shuddered. He made her feel unclean as his hand brushed near her breast.

'I *said*—' she ground her heel onto his instep till he yelped and let go '—I need to see to the coffee. Alone.'

She was breathing heavily as she swung round, ignoring the whispered stream of swear words that burst from him.

Movement at the edge of her vision brought her up short.

Declan. Her heart gave a resounding thump.

He loomed in the doorway, bigger than ever. His face was a pale mask of fury and his scar stood out like a jagged warning. Beneath his tailored jacket, muscles bunched. His hands fisted as if he wanted to reach out and shake her.

Relief at being free of Daniel's grip dissolved as Chloe looked into those fierce eyes. She scented danger and the hairs on her nape rose.

Yet it wasn't fear she felt. It was anger.

'Chloe...'

Chloe refused to let him berate her for trying to seduce his guest. She was tired of being a scapegoat, condemned for what she'd never done.

Spinning on her heel, she shoved open the kitchen door.

When she emerged the guests had left the dining table and clustered in the sitting room. Instantly she located Declan at the far end of the room with an older man.

'He's quite something, isn't he?'

Chloe found a gorgeous brunette standing close, swaying a little on her needle-point heels. 'Sorry?'

'Declan.' The other woman, Sophia, waved her glass, sloshing wine perilously near her couture gown. 'I've known him for years and I've never met a better man. Or a sexier one, despite that horrible scar.'

She drained her glass. 'One thing about Declan, you can trust him. He's loyal and honest. Unlike some.' She looked daggers at a blond man in intimate conversation with another woman. 'And wasn't he wonderful with that snake Daniel?'

'Daniel?' Chloe looked again around the room. She'd expected another confrontation but hadn't seen him. 'Where is he?'

'You missed it?' Sophia waved her glass. 'I've never seen anything like it. Declan marched him off the premises by the scruff of his neck.'

'Declan did that?' Stunned, Chloe turned. Resplendent in formal clothes, Declan radiated charisma at odds with the wrathful man of just ten minutes ago. 'Are you sure?'

'Absolutely. Declan all but shoved him out the door. Goodness knows what he'd done.'

Something deep inside Chloe shuddered into life. Had he ejected Daniel for pawing her? The idea sucker-punched her. It was the strangest feeling to think he'd directed his scorching fury at her tormentor. That wasn't the action of an enemy. An enemy would have gloated.

Just then Declan's head snapped round, as so often in the past when he'd sensed her presence.

The air sizzled with a charge that electrified her. The gleam in his eyes held something other than the disapproval she expected. Something that confounded her. Something intense and almost possessive.

Flurries of heat danced across her flesh and her eyes widened.

She recalled his hoarse voice. *You were so convincing, you even made me...*

Every night those words circled in her brain. She'd heard his pain and despair and wondered if, against all logic, he *did* still feel something for her. It seemed impossible yet she couldn't dismiss it.

'Declan saw Daniel follow me and make a nuisance of himself.' The words escaped before she realised.

'See?' Sophia nodded. 'I told you he was one of the good ones.' She sighed. 'A shame I was never his type.'

With difficulty Chloe dragged her gaze from Declan's. She felt his stare like a touch. It drew her skin tight and filled her with an awareness that undermined her indignation and made a mockery of her anger.

It was still there, the connection between them that had ignited from the first. It was stronger than distrust.

She darted another look. His ebony eyes lingered on her, his brow puckered as if he, too, was at a loss. Could he be having second thoughts?

She'd told herself time and the easing of his grief might eventually allow him to see the truth. Lately they'd lived in a cautious truce. Was it possible he'd begun to see past his pain?

Her heart crashed against her ribs as excitement rose.

'He's looking,' Sophia purred. 'Maybe it's time to see if I was wrong about not being his type.' She strolled across the room with a walk that drew all eyes.

Hurriedly Chloe turned to a cluster of guests. But, as the visitors gradually departed, the tension inside knotted tighter. Sophia remained plastered against Declan, his arm around her waist as she teetered on impossible heels.

Chloe busied herself, locating handbags and wraps, saying farewell to guests and tidying. But the knot inside drew tighter. *Jealousy?* How could she be jealous if she no longer cared for Declan?

She turned back into the sitting room, only to slam to a halt on the threshold.

One hand grabbed the door jamb as her knees weakened.

Declan and Sophia, kissing. Sophia's arms twined round Declan's neck. Declan swinging her up into his arms and striding down the corridor to the bedroom, heedless of her jewelled sandals dropping to the floor.

Chloe pressed a hand to her gaping mouth. It didn't stop her gasp of raw pain.

Declan neared the end of the dim corridor where the master suite was. He didn't turn on a light but shouldered his way in, cradling Sophia.

In the stillness Chloe heard the snick of the bedroom door. Numbly she stared at the lilac stiletto heels that had tumbled on the floor. She sagged against the wall.

Declan and Sophia. Declan doing with Sophia all those wonderful things he'd shared with Chloe.

Her teeth began chattering and she hugged herself tight as reaction set in.

She'd tried to tell herself these past weeks it had just been sex between her and Declan. That it didn't mean anything, conveniently ignoring the fact she was anything but promiscuous and in all her life she'd been to bed with only two men. Two men who had moved her and touched her heart: Mark and then, against the odds, Declan. She'd assured herself it had been an appalling mistake but one she'd get over.

With a gasp of pain Chloe slid down the wall. She sat hunched, knees drawn in tight.

She couldn't pretend any more. She'd skirted the truth too long.

At Carinya she'd fallen in love with Declan Carstairs.

How could she get over that?

She tried to despise him. Yet, seeing him with his friends and colleagues, she knew he wasn't totally the ogre he'd acted with her. Many of the qualities she'd found so attractive in him were real. It hadn't all been a sham.

How much of his rage was driven by grief?

If only he could be that cold-hearted, vengeful bastard through and through. Then she could turn her back without a second glance.

Yet he was far more complex. She saw glimpses of *her* Declan again and again. That was what hurt most.

Now, whether wittingly or inadvertently, he'd found the perfect way to punish her for all those crimes she hadn't committed.

It took less than thirty minutes to pack.

Chloe was halfway to the foyer when a yell rent the air, curdling her blood. She froze, clutching her bag.

Silence thrummed loud with the beat of her racing pulse. Could she have imagined it? Impossible.

Yet equally impossible it had come from the master suite.

Chloe made herself enter the vast sitting room where Sophia's shoes lay, proof that Declan wasn't alone.

There it was again: an agonised roar that prickled her skin. Dropping her bag, she swung towards the bedroom wing. It was dark, no light under any door. No sound. Surely if there was anything wrong…?

Then she heard it, a mumbling gasp, the deep resonance of Declan's voice. Talking to Sophia, of course.

Chloe's lips tightened as she moved away. She didn't want to overhear their pillow talk. But again she froze as a yell blasted the night and iced her veins. There was such pain in that cry.

It was Declan. Why didn't Sophia do something?

Knowing she'd regret it, but unable to turn her back, Chloe turned the handle and pushed open the door to the master suite.

Moonlight painted the room in silvery light. The king-sized bed was a mess of rumpled sheets, twisted and torn free. Instead of a couple there was only Declan, spread eagled across the mattress. His lips moved and his bare chest heaved. His head turned from side to side.

'Adrian!' This time she was close enough to understand his raw cry of anguish.

Quick as thought, she stepped into the room and closed the door.

'No, Adrian. Don't!' Declan's head thrashed on the pillow, his shoulders heaving as if he fought to free himself from some terrible weight.

'Shh.' Chloe found herself beside the bed, looking down at a face distorted by anguish. 'It's all right.'

He didn't hear, just flung out an arm as if to thrust something away. Or to make a desperate grab. Her heart clutched.

'Nooo!' His cry was a barely audible keen of loss. 'Ade, no!'

Chloe put her hand on his shoulder, feeling the film of sweat on burning flesh. 'It's OK, Declan. It's a dream.'

Muscles rippled and flexed beneath her touch. He rolled towards her, capturing her hand tightly. But one look at Declan's face told her he hadn't woken.

The proud man she knew wouldn't want her to see him like this. Even in the gloom she could make out his spiky lashes clumped together, see the tears on his cheeks and feel the shudders racking his body.

'It's all right, Declan,' she whispered, bending close. 'It's over.'

But it wasn't. She'd known he grieved for his brother, but hadn't understood the full depth of his trauma.

Chloe thought of the small photo in Declan's study, a family portrait: Declan at around twenty with a devil-may-care smile; Adrian, years younger in school uniform, grinning up at his big brother. In the middle were their parents, dressed to the nines and smiling stiffly.

She'd been surprised by the photo. Then she'd done her maths and realised Charles and Maya Carstairs had probably died soon after that photo had been taken. Perhaps it was the last keepsake of their family. She'd picked it up, transfixed by what she saw. Declan, looking carefree as she'd never seen him. Adrian with hero worship in his eyes.

And now this—Declan, tormented by nightmares of his brother. To see him racked in agony tore at her heart.

He had so much anger inside. How much of that piercing fury was self-directed?

She'd known he blamed himself for not saving Adrian. But she'd had no idea the guilt ran so deep. That shone a different light on his actions.

'Chloe?'

Startled, she looked down. His eyes were shut. His grip on her hand had eased as had his breathing.

'Sweet Chloe.' He rolled over, trapping her hand between his cheek and the pillow. 'Stay.'

It should have been easy to jerk her hand away.

Yet looking at that ravaged cheek, seeing the wet trail down his scar and the lines furrowing his brow, Chloe couldn't do it. Seeing Declan stripped of everything but the emotion he hid from the world, she felt the turmoil that drove him.

Even now he found no rest, no solace.

'Please.' The whispered syllable was so soft she almost missed it.

But she heard and, in a moment of honesty, knew she couldn't leave like this. Not yet. Wearily she settled on the carpet, her hand trapped against his warm skin.

She understood too well the weight of grief and how it could twist into self-blame. Was it grief that made Declan cling so obstinately to his guilt and his belief in hers?

Ever since that confrontation the night of the party, he'd looked different. As strong as ever, yet haunted. Often when he was by himself she'd find him staring into space. He'd looked adrift. Alone. As if there was nothing to anchor him.

Was she crazy to think he needed her now more than ever?

With a sigh she leaned her head against the bed. She wouldn't be leaving today.

CHAPTER TWELVE

'DECLAN, you look like hell.'

'Thanks, David.' He felt like it too, after weeks sharing the penthouse with his cool, perfect housekeeper who kept him at arm's length in an uneasy truce. He missed Chloe's fire, her vivid personality, her body. Damn! No wonder he barely slept. 'Was there anything else or did you just drop by to comment on my appearance? And why haven't you gone home?'

'You need to see this.'

Declan scraped his hand across bleary eyes. He'd spent too long in the office trying to find peace in the familiar demands of business. It hadn't worked.

Nothing had worked.

There'd been no peace since he'd plunged into this nightmare where the woman he cared for had transformed into a calculating gold digger.

But *was* she? Circumstances said yes. The evidence said yes. Yet his instinct said no.

Instinct told him she was special, the woman

he'd believed in before he'd learned of her connection with Adrian.

Yet how could he trust his instinct when it had given no warning Ade was on the brink of self-destruction?

He scrubbed a hand across his face again, his mind once more turning down endless tracks of self-doubt, disillusionment and longing.

'Declan.'

He looked up. David stood in front of the desk, holding out a package.

'This has just been sent through. It was posted the week before Adrian's death.' He paused as Declan's head jerked higher, every muscle tensing.

'Some fool in the legal office has been sitting on it all this time. When news came through about Adrian, they weren't sure what to do with it.' His PA snorted his disgust. 'Fortunately someone finally decided to check what it was they were holding and sent it on.'

He held out the small, padded envelope.

For a moment Declan stared. Sent the week Adrian had died?

A shiver slithered down his backbone. Another note from his brother? This time—and it filled him with aching guilt to admit it—he wasn't in a hurry to read it.

Yet it wasn't Adrian's writing on the registered envelope. It was Chloe's.

His hands closed around the parcel, his pulse racing.

What now?

He tipped the envelope and something soft fell into his hand. A piece of paper slid to the desk. He turned it over: *Please return to Mr Adrian Carstairs.*

That was all. No signature, but he knew Chloe's writing. Hadn't he pored over the notes she'd taken for him at Carinya time and again, as if seeking a clue to her character in her handwriting?

Declan looked at the soft pouch in his palm. It was weighty yet small. He tore it open and tipped out the contents. His breath stalled as he took in a familiar green glow. He stroked hard, perfect facets.

Slowly, reluctantly, realisation dawned.

'Declan! Are you all right? Will I get a doctor?'

Declan raised his hand. 'I'm fine.'

'You're not. You're white as a sheet. Is it your leg?'

Declan shook his head, eyes still fixed on the contents of the package. 'I'm OK, David,' he lied. 'Why don't you pack up for the night? It's very late.'

His PA hesitated but finally Declan was alone. He turned the bracelet over. It was the most expensive piece in his mother's collection: huge emeralds of exquisite quality surrounded by myriad diamonds and flawless pearls. A stunning piece of jewellery worth a rajah's ransom.

Light dazzled off it and raw pain sliced through him.

If Chloe was a gold digger on the make, why would she return several million dollars' worth of jewellery?

Declan had a sickening feeling his instinct about her had been right. That he'd made a terrible mistake.

Chloe hurried across the marble and glass foyer of the apartment building, aiming to catch an early train to the mountains. It had been a long week since she'd seen Ted.

Exiting onto the pavement, she stumbled to a halt, eyes widening. A gleaming, low-slung car was pulled up at the kerb. Declan leant against it, arresting with his dark looks, casual leather jacket and long, nonchalantly crossed denim-clad legs. He was the picture of potent masculinity, his scar adding an undercurrent of intrigue and danger.

Chloe blinked and turned away, her pulse hammering. She had to stop responding to the sight of him. But it was easier said than done.

'Wait.' He straightened, staggering a fraction as he took his weight on his bad leg. Another step and he stood tall, as if that stumble had never happened.

Yet it stopped Chloe in her tracks. Declan had persuaded everyone that, apart from his facial scar, he was fully recovered. It was only in private, when he thought himself alone, that she sometimes noticed him limp at the end of a long day.

That reminded her of the other scars he carried, unseen, the grief that drove him and softened her contempt for his behaviour.

'What is it, Declan?'

'I'm going to Carinya. I can give you a lift to see your foster father.'

She swung round, meeting his shuttered gaze full on. He looked drawn, his features pared back to stark planes.

'How do you know that's where I'm headed?' Was he having her followed?

'It's your day off.' Her suspicion must have shown, for he shook his head. 'The concierge told me.'

'Why should we travel together?' True, they'd shared the penthouse for weeks, but as strangers.

The strain of it drew her nerves almost to breaking point.

Running away would have been the easy option, if only she'd been able to bring herself to do it.

He stiffened. 'It's only for an hour or so. I'll have you there much faster than the train so you'll have more time for your visit.'

He was right. She was travelling against the daily commute and instead of an express she'd be stopping at almost every station.

'Besides, I want to talk with you.'

Chloe crossed her arms. 'So talk.'

He shook his head, stepping back as a woman walking a pair of dogs with jewelled collars slowed to pass. Behind her came two men in suits and a jogger.

'Not here. We need privacy.'

He was right. But to be cooped up in his luxury car all the way to the Blue Mountains? Breathing in his familiar spicy scent that, to her chagrin, still sent awareness tingling through her?

'Chloe.' He took a step forward then stopped, his face unreadable. But he couldn't mask the rough edge of emotion in his voice. It sounded like a plea.

Her breath quickened. What did he want? To tell her he was ready to see the truth about her and Adrian? Wishful thinking. How could she expect him to believe the woman he'd slept with one night over the brother he'd known a lifetime? She had no tangible proof. Besides, grief didn't pass so easily, nor, in her experience, the need to blame.

Unless Declan was stronger than she'd been when she'd lost Mark.

Yet hadn't he ejected one of his dinner guests because he'd pawed her? If Declan despised her he'd have accused her of seducing Daniel, or left her to fend for herself.

'Please, Chloe.' His ebony eyes met hers and heat shivered through her, igniting again that spark of connection. How could it still be so strong between them?

Everything she'd learned from his friends and colleagues indicated Declan was fair and honest. That he was clear sighted and generous. Was there a chance he might finally accept the truth?

She feared she was hopelessly optimistic.

Yet she yearned still for the man she'd fallen in love with. Love was too precious to set aside as if it had never existed.

She owed it to herself, and him, to try one last time.

Nevertheless, she had to force herself to get into his car. She trembled as she brushed past him and felt the heat of his body. Declan had hurt her, flayed her pride and her self-respect, betrayed her trust. Even knowing the pain that drove him, it was hard to put herself in his hands.

They drove silently through the city, except for the low, purring growl of the car. Declan seemed in no hurry to talk. Chloe stared at the city streets, anything rather than watch his clean, powerful profile or his capable hands on the wheel.

They were on the freeway heading west when finally he spoke.

'Thank you for taking care of Sophia.'

Surprised, Chloe turned to watch him. 'It was no bother.'

Sophia had emerged rumpled and sheepish from the guest suite on the morning after the dinner party, well after Declan's early start at the office. She'd been appalled at her behaviour the previous night, drinking too much and flirting outrageously to spite her ex-partner.

'She's not usually so…impulsive.' Declan shafted a direct stare at Chloe.

'I gathered that.' Just as she gathered Declan had been gentle but firm in rejecting her. He'd swept her to a guest suite to sleep off the effects of alcohol and misery.

Some men would have accepted what Sophia offered, even knowing she was drunk.

But Declan had behaved honourably.

Chloe remembered Sophia's praise for him over a late breakfast; it echoed what she'd heard from David and his associates. All thought him a paragon; a dynamo in business and an upstanding man.

Only with her did he show a dark side. To have seduced her, slept with her, opened up all those emotions and hopes it had taken years to suppress and then reject her...

'I'm grateful to you.' Tension edged his voice.

'It was nothing.' Organising fresh clothes, providing a sympathetic ear—none of it had been any trouble.

He shot her a gleaming look she wished she could read then concentrated on swinging the car up the first wide sweep of the incline to the mountains. It hugged the ground and Chloe realised with a frisson of shock that, despite all that horsepower under the bonnet, she'd never felt safer.

She drew a deep, fortifying breath. 'Was that all you wanted to discuss?'

'No, not all.' Even to his ears he sounded terse.

Could he blame lack of sleep? He'd only had one decent night's sleep lately—the night of the party when he'd dreamed Chloe had come to him. He'd woken to a sense of peace that had made a mockery of his distrust.

But the real reason for insomnia was his conscience.

Chloe looked so fragile. Lately she'd been pale but today she seemed as delicate as hand-blown glass. She'd walked from the apartment building and his gut had tightened as he saw the tension in her slim frame and the way her mouth turned down as if with grim thoughts.

His fault. He'd caused her distress.

The knowledge ate like acid. He remembered her poise and dignity even when he'd heaped the burden of his own guilt on her. He'd lashed out viciously. His skin crawled at the memory of all he'd said and done.

Because he'd needed a scapegoat for his pain, he'd made her suffer.

His hands grew clammy on the wheel, his heart thudding roughly against his ribs.

'Declan?' The low cadence of her voice stroked like velvet.

Abruptly he signalled, pulled over to the side of the road and switched off the engine. His hands shook. Had he subconsciously chosen to speak to her as he drove so he wouldn't have to look her in the eye?

Inwardly, he cringed. Chloe deserved better.

Declan turned to face her, his gaze roving with a freedom he hadn't allowed himself in weeks.

'I owe you an apology.'

She stared mutely, her eyes wide pools of shock.

'I've treated you appallingly.'

'You have.' Her brow pleated as if she didn't quite believe what she was hearing. Who could blame her?

'I acted out of shock.' And, he admitted now, out of sheer green-eyed jealousy. Some champion he'd been for Adrian. All this time he'd been jealous of his brother.

'I don't understand. What, exactly, are you apologising for?'

Chloe sat stiffly, obviously unwilling to take his words at face value. He reached out for her unresisting hand. It felt firm and capable, marked by work yet slender and feminine. His fingers closed tight around it.

'Everything.' He dragged a huge breath into his constricted lungs.

'I said I'd slept with you because I knew you'd betrayed Adrian. That my sight had come back and I wanted to test how easily you'd give yourself to a man with money who could make life easy.'

She tried to tug back her hand but he gripped it

in both his, not flinching from her glare. He deserved her wrath.

'You were despicable.'

'I lied, Chloe.'

'What?'

Part of him wanted to find hope in the fact she looked so stunned. As if she couldn't believe him guilty of an untruth. After all he'd put her through…

'I lied. Out of fury and shock. I despise myself for it. I lashed out because I was angrier than I'd ever been in my life and I wanted to inflict some of the hurt I was feeling.'

'On me.' Fire blazed in her eyes. He almost welcomed it after her cool distance.

He nodded. 'On you. I'm sorry.' He drew another mighty breath and laid the truth before her. He'd never behaved so badly in his life and he'd regretted it ever since, especially when he saw the pain in her eyes.

'I went to bed with you because I was desperate for you. *That's all.* There was no plot, no test.' His hold tightened. 'I wanted you, Chloe, as I've never wanted any woman.' Her expression froze in disbelief.

'Just the sound of your voice or a hint of your fragrance as you passed turned me hard with need.'

Declan's blood heated now, merely from touching her hands. For weeks he'd kept his distance, fearing what might happen if he got too close to the woman who stirred such strong reactions.

'I was trying to keep a lid on what I felt.'

Chloe scrutinised Declan's drawn face, reading regret and shame. His big frame tensed as if awaiting rejection. His hands on hers were firm but the tiniest of tremors passed through them.

Fear.

That was what she read in his face. Not just guilt and regret but, remarkably, fear.

Why? Fear she wouldn't forgive him?

Surely that couldn't be. Yet her heart tumbled hard as she grappled with this new Declan.

'I didn't regain my sight till after we'd slept together.' The admission sucked the breath from her lungs.

'The next day I recognised you from Adrian's photo. I was a coward.' He halted, grimacing. 'I didn't want to face you so I left.'

'Really?' She hardly dared believe. It had been bad enough to face Declan's accusations but worse by far had been the belief he'd deliberately seduced her in a tawdry test of character. Even now, the idea of being used like that sent a shiver of shame through her.

'You made me feel cheap.'

'I'm sorry, Chloe, more than I can say.' He leaned in, his voice urgent. 'I should never have let you believe it, even for a moment.'

'No,' she whispered, reliving the terrible searing pain of betrayal. 'You shouldn't.'

'There's no excuse for what I did. All I can say is that I regret it. That I'd do anything to make it up to you.'

Chloe stared. Declan was so intense, his words obviously heartfelt.

A tiny flicker of light flared in her battered heart.

'Why tell me now?' Steadfastly she concentrated on his words, not the feel of his strong hands enfolding hers or the fact she hadn't tugged hers away. She'd yearned for him to see the truth. Could her hopes be coming true?

'I couldn't lie any longer.'

His gaze seared hers. 'I've had doubts from the first. Every time I lashed myself into a fury about what you'd supposedly done I remembered how you'd been with me. Not seeking anything, just being yourself, caring and supportive, but always your own woman. I saw you interact with my friends. I saw your poise and strength in the face of my accusations, the way you rose above the worst of my behaviour.'

The naked emotion in his now unguarded eyes stunned her. He really meant it.

Could she forgive him? Her heart thudded faster.

'Then last night something happened that made me confront everything I thought I knew about you.'

His thumb stroked her palm, sending shivers of delicious sensation tingling through her.

She shouldn't let him touch her. He'd hurt her so badly. Yet she longed for his tenderness. Even now, trying hard to keep her distance, she relished his gentle caress almost as much as the salve of his words.

'Tell me.' Her nerves stretched taut in mingled expectation and fear of disappointment.

'The bracelet arrived. The one you returned.'

Chloe frowned. 'But I posted that to Adrian months ago. The day after I left Carinya. I'd told him I couldn't accept it,' she added quickly. 'But when I unpacked my things I found it stowed amongst my jewellery.'

She shuddered, remembering the shock of seeing it amongst her meagre collection of earrings. Adrian had obviously ignored her refusal and felt no qualms about rifling through her belongings to place it where he believed it belonged.

Declan shrugged. 'It never reached him. It got

delivered to the firm's legal office and then news arrived of his death.' His voice hollowed but he continued. 'Some junior clerk sat on it, wondering what to do with it. I received it just last night.'

He leaned closer, his gleaming eyes intent.

'It's worth a fortune. If you'd been a gold digger trying to get wealthy from the Carstairs brothers you'd never have returned it.'

'I *told* you I wasn't interested in your money.' Her mouth firmed.

'I know.' He swallowed hard. 'I'm sorry, Chloe. Sorry for all the hurt I've caused. All along I've wished—' He broke off, shaking his head.

'So you believe me now?'

'I believe you.' His deep voice made it a pledge.

A shimmer of excitement rose within her. She'd never seen Declan look so earnest, yet she needed the words.

'Tell me.'

Declan looked into her clear green eyes and felt himself slide into temptation. How badly he needed her. He'd always needed her. Yet he forced himself to continue, not pull her to him as he'd dreamed of doing so long.

'I know you never schemed for money. I know you never deliberately enticed me or Adrian.'

Her natural warmth and generosity were enough

to attract any man. Look at the way his guests had hung on her every word.

'I know you're honest and that I hurt you. Badly.'

His heart hammered as he watched emotions flit across her neat features. He stroked her hand possessively. He told himself he'd stop in a moment, that he'd just allow himself one final touch.

'I apologise, Chloe. Even knowing how your relationship with Adrian affected him, I was wrong to blame you. No one could have foreseen…'

'What did you say?' She stiffened.

'What happened wasn't your fault.' It might tear him apart to think of her with Ade but that was his problem, not hers. 'Obviously he was vulnerable with the loss of everything he'd worked for. He must have built up unreal expectations of his relationship with you—'

'His relationship with me?' Her voice held an odd, detached note.

He hurried to reassure her. 'I understand, Chloe. Adrian was good-looking and charming. You weren't to know he was…unstable.' Even now the word dried his mouth as if he'd swallowed ashes.

'I told you I wasn't your brother's lover.'

'It's OK, Chloe. I don't blame you.' If anyone was to blame it was Declan. He was Adrian's brother. He should have made it his business to check on him in person, not rely on long distance calls while he finished his business overseas. He should have done so much more.

'You still think Adrian and I had an affair?'

Declan frowned. 'I know you did. Adrian said so. He took photos of you in bed.' Bile rose at the memory.

Chloe yanked her hand free and shrank against the door. Her face turned milk-white.

'I *told* you, they were taken without permission. He came to my room and took photos while I slept. I felt *unclean* when I saw what he'd done.'

Declan shook his head. 'Don't. Please.' His gut twisted. Couldn't she just accept that he understood? Why continue to deny it?

'I've never lied to you, Declan.'

He gazed into her clear eyes and regret welled. His heart thumped a discordant beat and tension sank its talons into his flesh.

He didn't want this. He was trying to do the right thing.

When she spoke again her voice was leaden, like the cold weight in his belly. 'Why will you believe everything else, but not that? Why insist Adrian and I were lovers?'

Declan shut his eyes, his sinews stiffening and hands clenching into iron fists. He wished he could shut out the pain in her voice. Wished he could shut out the crushing weight of hurt inside.

'*Why*, Declan?' Her demand snapped his eyes open and he drank in the sight of her pain. Anguish filled him.

He was torn asunder between the two people who'd meant most to him.

He'd failed them both and he couldn't make it right.

Declan shied from her touch as she reached for him. Ice clamped his nape and chilled his veins.

'*Because it's that or believing the worst of Adrian.*' The words grated out. His heart catapulted against his ribs as he confronted the unthinkable.

'I either accept that he had an affair that went wrong, or…' he hefted a difficult breath into lungs that didn't seem to work any more '…believe the brother I knew and loved was a stalker who made you fear for your life.' Declan's voice cracked as pain splintered inside.

He dragged an unsteady hand through his hair. His chest felt like it would explode from the strain of holding in erupting emotions.

'You ask me to believe my kid brother turned into a *monster*?' He shook his head. 'I knew him, Chloe! That wasn't Adrian.' His fist thumped the console and pain streaked through him, but not enough to counteract the horror he faced.

'I know I frightened you with my accusations that you drove him to suicide. I overreacted, so of course you didn't want to admit the relationship.' The words scraped from his dry throat. 'But I can't believe the worst of him.'

Depression was one thing. Victimising an innocent something entirely different. That was *not* his brother.

Through a haze he eventually registered Chloe's stricken expression. Slowly she unclipped her seatbelt. Her gaze was dimmed, cloudy, as if some inner light had died.

His fault, his conscience screamed. No matter how hard he tried to make it right, his miasma infected her too.

'You're grieving, Declan. You feel you're to blame for his death. You're letting grief and bitterness blind you.'

Declan groped for a response but words were beyond him. He held himself together only by sheer will power.

She leaned nearer. Declan was hemmed in, trapped by her gaze and the words he didn't want to hear.

'I know what I'm talking about. I felt like that for

a long time when my husband died—that it was my fault for not realising sooner he should be in hospital. That it was down to me he'd died. Or, if not me, the hospital staff.'

'This isn't the same.' He could barely get the words out. One unwary move and he'd crack in two.

'It is.' The subtle scent of vanilla filled his nostrils, teasing him with Chloe's nearness. 'Until you face your guilt and grief, they'll never let you go. They'll tie you up so your emotions grow stunted and you find yourself living a half life. That's what happened to me.'

She lifted her hand to him. Her fingers stopped mere centimetres from his cheek and he sucked in a laboured breath. If she touched him…

'You've got enough scars from that day.' Her gaze rested on the stiff line of scar tissue that was an ever-present reminder of his failure. 'Don't carry more than you need to.'

Moments ticked by, measured by the searing pain of each breath as her gaze searched his face and he fought for strength against the temptation of her words.

He didn't deserve absolution. She asked too much. If he'd been a better brother, Ade would still be alive.

Finally he shook his head. 'Finished?' The word reflected all the searing pain within.

Her hand dropped. 'No.' She regarded him steadily. 'I don't hate your brother for what he did, though he scared me. I feel sorry for him. He was ill.' She paused. 'But most of all I feel sorry for *you*, Declan, because you're too scared to let go and see what's before your eyes.'

Chloe's mouth twisted. 'I love you, Declan. That's what you're too blind to see.'

Declan's heart missed a beat as he stared into her taut features. Surely he was hearing things?

'I cut myself off from the world because of grief and because I was too scared to leave myself open to hurt again.' Her words were so soft he had to strain to hear. 'But you came along and *provoked* me into love. *Seduced* me into it. And I can't crawl back into my safe little world again.'

Chloe's voice wobbled and he wanted to reach out and ease the pain written across her face. Pain he'd put there.

His fingers stretched out but she leaned away, as far from him as possible.

'I told myself I stayed out of pride but it was because I loved you, Declan. I couldn't leave knowing how much pain you were in, not when there was a chance I could make you see the truth.'

She hefted in a shuddering breath that tore at his soul. 'But my love isn't enough, not in the face of your distrust.' She spread her palms wide.

'I had no self-esteem as a kid, Declan. I was in foster care because my mum was a heroin addict who sold herself on the street for her next fix. I have no idea who my father was.'

Declan's heart cracked wide. 'Chloe—'

'No.' She raised an imperious hand. 'It took a long time and a lot of love for me to begin to believe in myself. To see that I was worth loving. And I *am*.' Her chin tilted in that familiar way that made his heart clench.

'I've loved you, Declan, but you're no good for me. I need a man who believes in me unquestioningly. A man who knows I don't lie. Not a man who thinks trusting me means disloyalty to his dead brother. I need a man who wants me, even when there's no proof I'm innocent except my word.'

The words slammed into him like projectiles, piercing him to the core. *Because they were true.*

He'd been so wrapped up in his pain he'd hurt Chloe, even when he tried to do the right thing. Even with proof that she was the woman he'd first believed her to be, he'd clung to what was safe. What was comfortable—for him.

What sort of caring was that?

He opened his mouth to speak but she was too quick.

'I'll find my own way from here.' Her tone stopped his instinctive grab for her. She snatched up her bag and pushed open the door. Her poise was brittle but determined.

'Don't come looking for me, Declan. *Ever.* It's over. I never want to see you again.'

CHAPTER THIRTEEN

CHLOE stared at the manager's name plate on the door and pushed back her shoulders.

It was a week since she'd left Declan and still the world reeled out of focus around her.

She'd been right to leave him. It would have been self-destructive to stay.

So why did everything feel wrong? Pain paralysed her when she thought of his anguish and grief; whenever she thought of never seeing him again. She might have done the right thing but it felt like part of herself had been wrenched away in the separation. Part of her that belonged with him.

But the world went on. Taking a fortifying breath, she knocked and was invited to enter.

'Ms Daniels.' The manager looked up with a smile. 'This is a pleasure. You've saved me a call. I was planning to contact you about your foster father's care.'

Chloe's heart plunged. 'That's why I'm here.'

At the other woman's invitation she slid into a

chair facing the desk. The office, like everything else in the facility, was welcoming and well cared-for. It would be hard to move Ted from here but she had no choice. With no reliable income she couldn't afford it. Having emptied her savings to install Ted here, it was all she could do to keep a roof over her head in the tight rental market in the mountains. She'd discovered jobs were at a premium as well.

'I wanted to warn you, Ted will be moving,' she blurted out, her chest cramping with pain at what she had to do.

'Really?' The other woman's eyebrows stretched up. 'I don't understand.'

Chloe licked her lips, preparing to explain, but the manager continued before she could speak. 'I thought you were happy with the care here, especially after receiving this.' She picked up a paper from a neat pile.

'I'm sorry?' Chloe frowned. 'I don't understand.'

Wordlessly the manager passed over the paper. Letterhead danced before her eyes as she tried to focus. A familiar name appeared at the bottom of the page: David Sarkesian had signed it on Declan's behalf.

Heart pounding, Chloe stiffened in her seat, scanning the text. She gaped.

'Declan Carstairs is footing the bill for Ted's care?'

'And for any extra therapy or medical expenses.' There was a pause. 'You didn't know?'

Dumbfounded, Chloe re-read the missive. 'I had no idea.'

What did it mean? Why should Declan pay the expenses of a man he'd never met?

'Well.' The other woman's voice grew brisk. 'I hope perhaps that changes your plans. The occupational therapist has seen promising changes in your foster father and wants to expand his program. I have the details here.'

Declan stared out onto the vast lawn between Carinya's shrubberies and the pool.

In his mind's eye he watched a chubby boy race across the grass, his grin triumphant as he retrieved a ball and hurled it at the cricket stumps.

This was where he'd taught Adrian to play cricket, in those endless, dry summer holidays while their parents had been busy making more money and socialising in the city.

He could almost hear the plock of ball against bat, the crow of delight as Adrian mastered his drive. The same triumphant cry he'd given when he'd perfected his tennis serve on the gravel court around the side, after weeks of Declan's coaching. Or when, sinuous as an eel, he'd learned to somersault into the pool, creating a splash that would wet any unwary bystander.

Declan's mouth tilted up. Ade had always been utterly focused on each new achievement to the exclusion of all else. It was a trait that ran strong in the Carstairs men.

But in Adrian, had that strength also been a weakness? How easily had that tendency for tunnel vision morphed into obsession with a woman, with a fantasy? Had it been easier to lose himself in that than face the destruction of the life he'd devoted himself to for years?

Declan's smile faded as he recalled his recent conversation with Ade's ex-business partner in London. A woman who, he'd discovered, had rose-gold hair and ivory skin like Chloe. A woman who'd clammed up when asked about Adrian's personal life, but who had admitted she'd been disturbed by his mood swings and increasing despondency.

Declan shoved his hands in his pockets, fists tightening. Had Adrian fallen for *her*, the woman he'd worked closely with, and who was now so recently wed to a wealthy banker? Had Chloe merely been a reminder of the lover who'd dumped him?

She could have been a convenient focal point for his thwarted feelings.

Declan would never know.

He wished things had been different. That he'd been able to intervene before Adrian had self-destructed. That regret would stay with him. But at least now he saw beyond it.

Turning, his belly tightened as he surveyed the spotless kitchen. Even empty it was full of Chloe's presence. He'd never seen her in this room, but like every other room in his home it was full of memories.

He only had to close his eyes to hear her husky laugh as she argued with him over how much chilli was too much in his favourite curry. To smell the sugar and yeast aroma of her baking and the even more delectable vanilla-and-sunshine scent that was pure Chloe. He felt warmth, not from the sun's rays, but from her presence.

He'd been happy. It was here he'd first faced his desire to be with her. Was that why he'd rejected so violently any hint his sight was returning? Because change might threaten their fragile relationship?

He'd hated the dark world of blindness but now… He surveyed the kitchen and emptiness welled.

Now with his sight and vigour returned, secure in his world once more, he knew a desolation that tormented him and turned his haven into a soul-less place. He longed for just one day without sight, basking in Chloe's no-nonsense care, her tender concern, her love.

He'd had her love and he'd destroyed it.

His heart hammered and the bitter taste of self-disgust filled his mouth. He'd thrown away the most precious thing in the world, shoved aside the woman he should have cherished, not vilified.

Hearing about her past, he'd been stunned by her strength and resilience and shamed by the knowledge of how he'd treated her.

She was right to have left him.

She was better off without him.

He didn't deserve her.

Yet how could he go on without Chloe?

He spun on his heel and strode out the door.

CHAPTER FOURTEEN

CHLOE widened her stance on the tiled floor, trying to concentrate on the latest dinner orders. But her head was muzzy with exhaustion and her limbs felt heavy, aching with tiredness. Heat and the pungent odour of deep-fried food pressed down on her and in a sudden wave nausea hit again.

Staggering, she reached for the water she kept handy. There was a crash, glass splintering across the floor and she grabbed desperately for the worktop, trying to keep her balance rather than step into the shattered glass.

Her breath came in shallow pants as she fought back bile and tried to steady her spinning head.

'What's going on here?' An angry baritone thundered from the door to the café's dining room.

Great. Just great. Chloe squeezed her eyes shut, trying to summon strength to deal with her irate employer. He'd been in a foul mood all day, particularly since her replacement for the afternoon shift hadn't turned up, and he'd been taking out his ire on the overworked staff.

If she didn't need this job so badly, she'd have walked weeks ago.

She urgently needed to put away some savings plus she had to repay Declan for Ted's care. She hadn't been proud enough to reject his offer to foot that bill. But she was proud enough not to want to be beholden to him in the long term. She couldn't afford any ties to Declan.

'I *said*,' her boss bellowed, 'What's going on here?'

Slowly she turned, forcing herself to stand tall, though every muscle in her body ached. She slid one hand over her empty stomach, trying to force down the need to retch in the thick, fat-filled air of the kitchen.

'Just a broken glass.' She looked down at the shards littering the floor and realised she hadn't a hope of gathering them up. One unwary move and she'd either collapse or lose her battle with welling nausea.

'I really need to leave,' she found herself saying again. Only this time she'd make him understand. 'My shift finished five hours ago and I'm exhausted.' Not to mention she'd started the day well before that, cooking breakfasts in her other job in the kitchens of the mountains' most exclusive guesthouse. 'If I stay on, there are bound to be more accidents.'

'Stop making excuses.' He crossed beefy arms over his chest. 'There's no one else to cook. Just get on with it.'

Chloe stifled a protest. She knew half a dozen other staff who'd willingly work the extra hours. But she suspected he'd have to pay them more. She'd been so desperate to find a job locally she'd only just begun to question her very low wage. Had he read her desperation and taken advantage of it?

She untied her apron with fumbling fingers, then drew it over her head.

'I told you, I can't. I'm making too many mistakes. It's dangerous.' The sound of sizzling fat underscored her words and she turned to rescue an order of fish and chips.

'Walk out on me and you lose your job,' he snarled.

Chloe faltered, her flesh chilling at his threat. She needed this income so badly.

He paced towards her and automatically she stepped back into the corner. The look in his eye frightened her. She knew his temper…

'Lay a finger on her and you'll wish you'd never been born.' The lethally soft voice cut the thick air.

Chloe's head whipped round towards the door and shock froze her. Declan? Was she dreaming about him when she was awake now, as well as in her sleep?

Her boss dropped his beefy arm and swung round.

'Who the hell are you?'

Declan stepped into the kitchen, letting the swing door close behind him. Instantly the room shrank. 'I'm the man who'll see you treat Ms Daniels right.'

Two more steps and he stood toe-to-toe with her boss. He looked down into that florid, choleric face while the other ranted.

'Enough.' One powerful hand sliced through the air and, remarkably, her boss's tirade stopped. Chloe swayed and groped for support.

Ebony eyes cut to her, seeming to take in everything from her stained black trousers and fitted T-shirt to the feelings she couldn't hide: disbelief, excitement and sheer exhaustion.

Declan's voice, glacial as she'd never heard it, penetrated her hazy brain: words like 'assault', 'threatening behaviour', 'exploitation', 'official reports'…

She told herself she could fight her own battles.

She'd been doing that all her life, but right now merely staying upright was challenge enough.

'Don't move.' His voice pulled her up short when she would have shuffled to one side.

Looking down, she saw Declan's dark head, his long fingers gathering up wickedly sharp fragments of glass and depositing them in an old container.

The scene seemed unreal. If she dropped one hand she'd touch his thick, dark hair, feel the strength of his broad shoulder beneath her palm.

Chloe wanted to so badly. She blinked back hot tears as emotions bombarded her. Why couldn't he stay away as she'd demanded? It didn't matter that she'd regretted it ever since. That despite the need for self-preservation she didn't feel *whole* without Declan.

She'd saved her sanity and her self-respect but in leaving him she'd left part of herself behind.

'Don't cry, Chloe.' His voice was husky and his eyes fathomless as he looked up at her.

She blinked and stiffened her spine.

'I never cry.' It was true. She was strong. She'd had to be. It was just that she was so very tired.

'Where is he?' There was no one else in the room. Just her and the man crouched at her feet.

'Don't worry about him.' In one easy movement

Declan rose and deposited the glass in the bin. Then, before she could guess his intent, swung her up into his arms.

She protested, of course. Chloe wouldn't put up with being manhandled without a fight.

But now he had her safe in his arms, he couldn't let her go. His hold tightened.

He remembered her cringing away from her bully of an employer and it had red-rimmed his vision. He'd wanted to beat the guy into a pulp. Only the realisation Chloe would then have to face police interviews kept him sane. Instead he'd threatened the lowlife with legal action for everything from aggressive behaviour to shonky employment practices, non-adherence to council bylaws and health regulations.

Declan held her close as they negotiated the door from the café to the pavement. She'd lost weight. She'd looked so small and defenceless back there, despite her defiant stance. Now he felt the press of her hip bone rather than the lush curve he remembered.

'Haven't you been eating?'

'What?' She broke off her protests and stared up at him.

Heat punched low in his belly as her green eyes

met his. His breath stalled in his lungs as he fell into those crystal depths.

He'd longed to see her, to touch her. But not like this. Not with violet bruises under her eyes and her too-thin arms wrapped around herself as if to protect her even from him.

He opened the car with a click of the remote control. 'You haven't been eating. What were you thinking?'

Eyes rounded, she stared up at him as if he spoke another language. He took advantage of her silence to manoeuvre her into the car and strap her in.

'What are you doing? I never said I'd go with you.'

But her movements were slow and uncoordinated. He was in the car, its engine purring as he nosed it onto the street, before she could unclip the catch on the seatbelt.

Ten minutes later her protests had died to mulish silence as he pulled up under the *port-cochere* of an exclusive guesthouse.

'What are we doing here?'

'I'm staying here.' He vaulted out of the car and opened her door before the staff could reach it, unsnapped her seatbelt and pulled her into his arms while she goggled at him.

'Put me down,' she hissed. 'I can't go in here like this. I *work* here.'

Declan suppressed a smile of satisfaction. He revelled in the feel of Chloe in his embrace, though he knew it was a fleeting delight. He'd take whatever crumbs he could get.

The thought of the emotional wasteland that was his life without her wiped the smile from his face. But he pulled her closer, as if daring any of the staring guests and staff to try separating them.

He even enjoyed the sensation of her turning her face into his shirt, the warmth of her breath against him, though he realised she was merely avoiding curious looks.

She felt so *right* in his arms.

He could have held her for hours, but too soon they were at his room. He shouldered his way in and let the door slam shut before striding across to a lounge suite in front of a balcony with an unparalleled view of the escarpment.

Reluctantly he put her down on the cushioned lounge, then stood, his blood sizzling in reaction, his breathing shallow not from exertion but emotion.

She was gorgeous, even in stained work clothes and with exhaustion stamped on her too-fine features.

Abruptly he turned and poured a glass of chilled water from a nearby carafe. She took it without comment but his belly clenched as she carefully avoided touching him.

'What do you want to eat?' His voice was gruff, not what he'd intended.

Fine eyebrows arched up. 'I'm not staying.'

She'd stay till he made sure she never went back to that café or any place like it. Till she promised...

His breath hissed out as he realised he had no right to demand anything from Chloe.

'I'll order some food.'

'I don't want food. I feel sick.'

Declan hesitated, noticing her pallor did have a sickly hue. She needed looking after.

'Humour me, Chloe. You look like you're about to pass out.' His gaze held hers till she looked away. 'I'll order a selection. Hopefully you'll find something to tempt your appetite.' He busied himself with the call to room service, trying to quell the need to haul her to him and never let her go. Her words still rang in his ears.

It's over. I never want to see you again.

He ended the call and turned towards her. She was where he'd left her, hunched at one end of the vast sofa staring out of the window. Her bare arms were too thin, the elegant line of her throat too fragile. The only rounded part of her was the tiny belly she rubbed with one hand.

A flash of memory smote him: Chloe in the café, backing away from her irate boss. There'd been fear in her eyes but instead of putting up a hand to ward him off her fingers had splayed protectively over her abdomen.

A stifled sound made Chloe whip her head round. Declan stood as if transfixed. His eyes gleamed as he raked her body. Self-consciously she slipped her hand from her tummy and reached again for the water.

Her teeth still chattered a little against the glass but she felt stronger. Much as she hated to admit it, being swept off her feet and into Declan's luxury car, carried through the exclusive resort as if she were breakable porcelain, had been like a pleasurable dream. A dream where mistakes and hurt didn't exist and where Declan came to her free of the past.

But dreams weren't reality.

'What are you doing here, Declan?'

He paced closer.

Too close, screamed the voice of sanity.

Yet her eyes ate him up. His tanned, bold features, the ebony hair, the liquid dark eyes, even the scar that raked his cheek—all were shatteringly familiar.

Part of her wanted to push him away so he didn't crowd her. The other part insisted he wasn't close enough. She locked her fingers around the glass lest they reach for him. Liquid slid down her parched throat. Still their eyes meshed, as if neither could believe the other was real.

'I came to see you.' His voice had an odd inflection. 'How long have you been feeling sick?'

Chloe shrugged. 'I've been working long hours in a stuffy kitchen, that's all.' She put the glass down and swung her legs to the floor. 'I really need to—'

'You're pregnant, aren't you?' His eyes glittered as they roved her and she froze.

How had he known? She barely showed. He *couldn't* know. She was only coming to terms with the news herself. She wasn't ready to discuss it with Declan.

'I'm just tired. Thank you for your help back there, but it's better if we don't see each other again.' She forced the words from her lips though she was no longer sure they were true. Just as she was no longer sure she'd been right telling him it was over between them.

Gingerly she stood.

'When is our baby due, Chloe?' The hoarse intensity of his voice sent a thrill zipping down her spine.

'*Our* baby?' In her wildest dreams she'd never imagined he'd call it that. Those simple words confounded her.

Like lightning his gaze lifted to hers, pinioning her.

'Our baby.' His tone held a quality she'd never heard before. It made something deep inside her clench. 'Don't worry; I can work out the dates myself.'

'What makes you think it's yours?' She lifted her chin and dared him to repeat it. He'd spent too long distrusting her.

'It's mine.' The look he bestowed her sent the blood hurtling through her veins and a flush seared her face. 'Yours and mine, Chloe.'

'You don't know that.' Bitterness filled her. 'Not so long ago you accused me of being a woman on the make. A woman who'd—'

His fingers across her lips stopped her words, their soft pressure a tantalising restraint. Chloe drew a shuddering breath and looked away, blinking as his hand dropped.

'Don't, Chloe.' His voice, low and hoarse, was strained.

'Why not?' She swung back to face him. 'You used condoms. There's nothing to prove this is your child. I could have gone to someone else's bed when I left you.'

Slowly he shook his head. 'I'm sorry for mistrusting you. If there was a way to take back what I said, I would.' He breathed deep and she watched his massive chest rise. 'You told me you loved me. You'd never sleep with someone else while you still felt like that. Not you.' His dark eyes bored into hers. 'You don't use sex for recreation, do you, Chloe? It's too important. It's about feelings, isn't it?'

It's about love, she wanted to say, but the words choked in her throat. How could Declan, the man who'd misjudged her so long, see right to the core of her?

This new Declan made her feel vulnerable, unsure of herself, as if he'd shifted the ground beneath her feet. He'd changed.

'It could be anyone's. Even—'

'It's not Adrian's.'

'How can you be sure?'

His lips curved in a sad smile. 'You told me, remember?'

Stunned, she groped for words. She searched

his face and saw only certainty there. 'You didn't believe me.'

Declan shook his head again. 'I did.' He reached out his hand as if to touch her then let it fall. His mouth turned down, his skin pulling tight, sharpening his features as if under severe stress.

'I listened to everything you said and I knew it was true. I hid behind accusations so I wouldn't have to face the truth. I was a coward.' He shook his head. 'It was hell letting you walk away that day, but I knew I had no right to ask you to stay. I'd hurt you too badly. You were right—I was no good for you.'

And now? The words trembled on her tongue. But it was no use wishing for a fairy tale ending. This was real life.

She struggled to take in the change in him.

'I'm sorry for what I said that day. I know you were grieving.' The knowledge of his misery, so like her own past grief, allowed her to understand his obstinate loyalty to his brother, even when he'd hurt her.

'No. You were right, Chloe. You deserve a man who can be everything you need. Everything I wasn't. I can only apologise again for the appalling way I treated you.'

He speared his fingers through his hair. The infinite sadness in his expression made her heart clench.

'Adrian's actions were his own. You were never the cause of his pain. You were a victim.' He swallowed hard. 'I'm sorry.'

Declan's desolation confirmed what she'd known—that it was too late for them. A yawning void opened up between them and her heart plunged.

A knock on the door claimed his attention and Chloe turned and paced onto the balcony. The soft twilight wrapped round her. Out on the lawns a cluster of guests laughed and chatted. But here, alone with her thoughts, desolation crept in. She was glad Declan was finally able to face the past. Pleased he'd moved on from his grief. Yet still she wished...

A footfall behind her made her spin round. Declan's gaze dropped to her abdomen then up to her eyes. His lips curved in a smile that stole her breath.

'What are you smiling about?'

'You're having my child.'

Her skin tingled at his words. He was so *sure*.

His certainty rocked her after his previous mistrust. He'd only changed his mind about her before when he'd learned she'd returned the bracelet. This time there was no proof short of a DNA test.

'There's no proof it's your child.' She blurted the words out, as if tempting him to distrust her.

His smile didn't dim. She blinked. He undermined her certainties.

'How did you find me?'

'Ted.'

'You rang my foster father?'

'No, I saw him. I wanted to meet him because he means so much to you.'

Chloe's heart fluttered. The intensity of Declan's scrutiny unnerved her. She felt poised on the brink of a precipice, not knowing what to expect next.

'You paid for Ted's accommodation. I want you to know I'll pay you back every cent.'

'I don't want your money.' He shoved his hands deep in his pockets and his shoulders hunched.

'I don't want to owe you anything. I want to be free.'

His lips curled, yet there was no amusement in his face, just the echo of suffering. 'If you feel a fraction of what I do, Chloe, you'll never be free.'

What did he mean?

'Did Ted persuade you to see me?' She knew Ted was worried about her long working hours, not knowing it was the loss of Declan that was the real problem.

'We didn't talk about you.' At her disbelieving stare, Declan shrugged. 'Not after I explained who I was. Then we just…talked. About sport to start with and then his work on the railways.'

'You and Ted talked about trains?' Chloe sagged against the balustrade, struggling to take it in.

'Not just that. We touched on fishing, politics, working in China and the Middle East. He's an avid armchair traveller, your Ted.' Declan sounded approving, yet Chloe barely noticed. She was on tenterhooks, her tension growing with each revelation.

'Why are you here?'

Instantly Declan stiffened. 'I know you didn't want to see me, Chloe. That's why I kept away, but I needed—' He paused and looked down at the papers he drew from his jacket pocket. 'I had to give you this personally.'

Thick paper crackled as he handed it over. For an instant Chloe hesitated, then she forced herself to reach for it, feeling warmth where it had lain next to his body.

'What is it?' Slowly she unfolded it.

'The deeds to Carinya. I want you to have it.'

'What?'

She had to be hearing things. Yet the words on the top page suddenly began to make sense. Chloe stumbled a fraction then shot out a hand to support herself. When she looked up Declan was a mere pace away.

'You can't do that. Carinya is your family home. Wasn't it built by your great-great-grandfather?'

'I have no family now, Chloe.' At the grim twist of his lips, pain lanced her.

He turned and braced his hands on the balustrade. 'I want you to have it. I know you loved it and it will be a perfect place for Ted once he's ready.' Declan drew in a slow breath, his eyes fixed on the valley spread before them.

'I can't live there, Chloe.' His voice dropped to a deep resonance that tightened her skin. 'Every time I enter a room there, I smell your sweet fragrance. I hear you humming under your breath. I *want* you to be there.' He swung round to face her, his eyes glittering. 'It's not the same without you. I even moved out of my Sydney apartment. I was living in a hotel in the city before I came here.'

Chloe swallowed hard, seeing the emotion in Declan's eyes. He was letting her in, allowing her to read the feelings he usually kept shut away. It was heady and glorious and frightening.

'I can't accept—'

'You can, Chloe. I wronged you badly and made your life hell. It was easier to blame you than shoulder all the guilt for—'

'You're not to blame either.' Unthinkingly she put her hand on his sleeve and felt the muscle tense under her touch. She loosened her fingers to sever the connection but his other hand clamped hers in place.

Fire sparked in Declan's gaze and an answering heat flooded her.

'I'm still working on that one.' His smile was crooked and endearing and Chloe's heart flipped over.

'But this isn't about Adrian. After all you'd already been through, you deserved a champion. Not an accuser. I *hurt you*, Chloe.' His hand tightened and Chloe's pulse thudded faster as she read Declan's expression.

'I stayed away as long as I could. I visited your father because it was a connection to you. I reminded myself you never wanted to see me again.' He drew a deep breath. 'If you tell me to go now, I will and I'll never bother you again. But I had another reason for coming here.'

'Yes?' She could barely breathe over the tightness in her chest.

He hesitated so long she wondered if he didn't

know how to continue. Yet that wasn't possible. Not forthright, decisive Declan.

'I've been desperate since you left. I knew I couldn't follow you, though I wanted to, more than anything. You had a right to make a new life without me. But I can't let go so easily, Chloe. I just can't do it!' Emotion clogged his voice.

'Did you know you left in such a hurry you didn't pack everything? There were CDs still in the player and books on the shelf. Since you left I've listened to your music and read the books too.' At her startled stare, he nodded. 'Pathetic, isn't it? I've become a fan of Jane Austen and Latin salsa and, Lord help me, Aussie hip hop.'

'Declan?' Chloe's voice wobbled.

'Ah, sweetheart.' He palmed her cheek, infinitely tender. 'I'm sorry. I really have made you cry when all I want is to look after you.' He dragged in a breath so shaky it made her wonder if, impossibly, Declan felt as nervous as she.

'I don't need looking after.' She watched his lips curve in a smile that warmed her from the inside.

'I love you, Chloe. I have for so long, but I was too caught up in blaming you.' Chloe's heart stuttered at the tenderness in his eyes, then tripped to a faster beat.

'I wish there was a way I could prove it to you.

Prove I believe in you and always will, no matter what. Words aren't enough.' The gleam in his eyes dimmed and his mouth tightened.

'You did prove it,' she whispered, stunned by the realisation. The warmth within spread and intensified to a steady glow. 'You knew the baby was yours from the first, no matter what I said. *You believed in me.*'

His faith in her had been instantaneous. He'd *shown* her his change of heart.

With infinite care he brushed her hair behind her ear, letting his fingers linger in a delicate caress. Delight shivered through her. She stood unmoving, snared by what she saw in his eyes and what she felt.

'I love you, Chloe. For so many reasons. Because you stood up to me when I deserved it. You never let me railroad you into anything. You made me take a hard look at myself.' He pressed a kiss to the back of her hand and a ripple of heat sped through her.

'Because of the way your laugh always makes me smile, even when the world seems black and unforgiving.' Another kiss, this time to her wrist, drew her skin taut.

'Because of your sexy body and your soft skin

and the way you welcome a lover with all of you, body and soul.'

Chloe tried to pull back, but he held her firm and planted a kiss to the centre of her palm. 'Because you're honest and sincere. Because you had the generosity of heart to forgive my brother as I'm hoping you can forgive me.'

Her treacherous legs wobbled and he caught her close.

'I love you, Chloe. I have no right to expect you to love me, but I had to tell you. I've been a complete b—'

'Don't!' Her fingers sealed his lips as she found her voice again. It throbbed with all the emotion welling inside. 'I love you, Declan. Still. Always.'

The stunned look in his eyes made her smile.

'I love your intensity.' She held his gleaming gaze, reassuring him with everything in her. 'Your honesty and determination to do right. I love your loyalty.

'I love that you're a man of honour.' She suppressed a smile as she remembered jealousy over Sophia. 'And I love the way you make love to me.'

'I can't believe it.' He cradled her close, the look in his eyes something she'd carry with her the rest of her life. 'You make me feel invincible, even with *this*.' He lifted a dismissive hand to his scar.

'It's part of you, Declan. I even love that.' She smiled at his startled look. 'It gives you a swash-buckling air, like a marauding pirate.'

'Does it indeed?' He scooped her into his arms and held her close. 'You know what pirates do when they find beautiful wenches, don't you?' He strode from the balcony and across the room till he reached the huge bed.

Abruptly his grin faded and his grip tightened.

'I don't deserve you, Chloe. You'd have every right—'

Chloe stopped him in the most sensible way she knew. She tugged his head down and planted a breathless kiss on his mouth, opening for him, till with a groan he plunged in and took her with a thorough, ravishing kiss that made her head spin and her heart soar.

'The past is over, Declan,' she whispered. 'Let's concentrate on the future.'

'I'll spend our future showing you every day how much I love you.' The earnest light in his eyes and his tender smile were the most perfect things Chloe had ever seen.

EPILOGUE

CHLOE smiled as she turned the corner of the veranda and saw the impromptu football game on the lawn.

Ted's companion dog, a beagle crossed with no-one knew what, barked excitedly and pranced across the grass.

Amy, with all the fierce concentration of a two-year-old, tottered after the lightweight ball to where Ted guarded a goal of bright plastic buckets. He feinted to one side, pretending to use his walking stick to stop the ball. But anyone seeing the expression on his face knew he had no intention of spoiling his granddaughter's goal.

Amy kicked with such comical exaggeration that she fell over. But there were no tears, just a crow of delight when the ball slid past Ted.

'G'anpa, G'anpa! I did it.'

'I saw, sweetie.' Ted reached down and pulled her to her feet. Instantly she wrapped her arms around his legs.

Chloe's heart lurched as she watched her daughter and Ted together. She was so lucky to have them. So very lucky.

'They're good together, aren't they?' A deep, rich voice shivered across her skin as her husband stepped close, tugging her back against him.

'Hmm, hmm.' She smiled as he wrapped his arms around her and she sank into his familiar, warm embrace. 'They are.'

Declan's hands slipped down to her small baby-bump, caressing with a gentleness that always made her heart turn over.

'We're very lucky, my love.' He nuzzled her neck and sparks cascaded through her. Her nipples hardened and heat swirled deep within. 'I have to be the luckiest man alive.'

Chloe turned and wrapped her arms around his neck. She looked into his beloved face and read the love shining in his eyes. 'And I'm the luckiest woman.'

'You've got lipstick on,' he growled in mock anger.

'You expect me to go to the gala and not wear make-up? On the arm of the sexiest man there, who just happens to be the foundation chair?'

The foundation, named for Adrian, provided community support to people with mental illness.

Its focus was on filling gaps left by other services, rather than on glitzy events. This annual fundraiser was the exception, attended by a who's who that always made the celebrity pages.

'You could have waited.' Declan leaned close, a tell tale gleam in his eyes. 'But no matter. You can put more on later.'

His breath was warm on her face and her eyes had just fluttered shut when a small form cannoned into their legs.

'Mummy, Daddy, I goaled. Did you see? Did you see?'

'We saw, darling.' Chloe smiled as she watched Declan pick up their daughter and hug her. Amy hugged him back, planting grubby hands on his tuxedo and dress shirt.

'We might be a little late leaving for the gala,' Chloe murmured. 'You'll need to take that off.'

The look he sent her was a sizzle of pure invitation. 'Promises, promises, Mrs Carstairs. I look forward to you helping me.'

* * * * *

Mills & Boon® Large Print
August 2012

A DEAL AT THE ALTAR
Lynne Graham

RETURN OF THE MORALIS WIFE
Jacqueline Baird

GIANNI'S PRIDE
Kim Lawrence

UNDONE BY HIS TOUCH
Annie West

THE CATTLE KING'S BRIDE
Margaret Way

NEW YORK'S FINEST REBEL
Trish Wylie

THE MAN WHO SAW HER BEAUTY
Michelle Douglas

THE LAST REAL COWBOY
Donna Alward

THE LEGEND OF DE MARCO
Abby Green

STEPPING OUT OF THE SHADOWS
Robyn Donald

DESERVING OF HIS DIAMONDS?
Melanie Milburne

0712 Rom LP